William Edward Gilmore

Life of Edward Tiffin

First Governor of Ohio

William Edward Gilmore

Life of Edward Tiffin
First Governor of Ohio

ISBN/EAN: 9783337333584

Printed in Europe, USA, Canada, Australia, Japan

Cover: Foto ©Raphael Reischuk / pixelio.de

More available books at **www.hansebooks.com**

LIFE OF

EDWARD TIFFIN

FIRST GOVERNOR OF OHIO

BY

COLONEL WILLIAM EDWARD GILMORE

CHILLICOTHE, O.

HORNEY & SON, Publishers

1897

PREFACE

VERY nearly a century has elapsed since Edward Tiffin was inaugurated the first governor of the State of Ohio; and yet two of his children—Miss Diathea Tiffin and Mrs. Ellen Tiffin Cook, aged respectively eighty-three and-eighty-one—still survive; and in such state of health and vigor as render it not altogether unreasonable to hope they may yet live to celebrate the centennial of that event.

It is at the request of these two venerable and honored daughters of Governor Tiffin that this brief memoir has been prepared and published; and to them it is respectfully and affectionately inscribed by their kinsman,

WILLIAM E. GILMORE.

CHILLICOTHE, OHIO, *May* 1, 1897.

LIFE OF EDWARD TIFFIN

FIRST GOVERNOR OF OHIO

CHAPTER I

Parentage and Birth—Early Education—Begins the Study of
Medicine in Carlisle, England—Emigrates to America—
Resumes and Finishes Medical Studies—Marriage—Re-
ligious Impressions—Ordination as Deacon in Methodist
Episcopal Church—Manumits Negro Slaves—Removal
to Northwest Territory.

EDWARD TIFFIN was born in the city of Carlisle,
England, on the nineteenth day of June, 1766.

His parents, Henry Tiffin and Mary Parker, his
wife, were both of good descent and family connec-
tions, but possessed of no property of consequence ;
and Edward's education was principally provided
for by a generous maternal uncle, Edward Parker,
for whom he was named.

Mr. Samuel Williams, late of Cincinnati, Ohio,
who was for more than twenty years of his life
connected intimately with Governor Tiffin, by reason of serving him in the capacity of chief clerk

while Tiffin held the office of Commissioner of the General Land Office of the United States, and afterwards that of Surveyor-General of the North-west, in a paper published in Rev. J. B. Finley's *Sketches of Western Methodism* (1854), says that Tiffin's education " was limited to the ordinary branches of a common English course."

That Mr. Williams understates his educational accomplishments is abundantly apparent in Tiffin's subsequent career; for, although he was essentially a practical man, with his interest and industry absorbed in current affairs, without thought of posthumous fame as an orator, writer, or statesman —for he preserved no memorials of himself what-ever—all evidence that has come down to us proves that he always spoke readily, clearly, and effectively in debate ; and all his papers accessible now, including a few of the sermons he preached, are written in excellent style, in faultless English and admirable good taste.

The fact that he was a student of medicine be-fore he was eighteen years of age, and that he attained acknowledged eminence in this learned profession notwithstanding his many other employ-ments in life, almost conclusively proves he pos-sessed some knowledge of the Latin language, and considerable attainments in those other sciences which are essential to this profession.

In 1784 his parents, with their five children, of

whom Edward was third in the order of their birth, left England and chose an American home in Charlestown, in what was then Berkeley County, but since then included in the present county of Jefferson, in the State of West Virginia.

It has frequently been asserted that the subject of this memoir came to this country in the capacity of surgeon on a British man-of-war; that he was attached, as surgeon, to the army of Burgoyne and taken prisoner with that army; that he was held as such prisoner until the close of the war, and only then concluded to become an American citizen; and more to the same general effect. These stories all originated in an obituary sermon preached by a Methodist minister in 1829, and which sermon was printed in a newspaper of southern Ohio at the time.

The indisputable fact that he was born in 1766, and was, therefore, only eleven years old at the time of Burgoyne's surrender of his army, sufficiently refutes all these statements.

Immediately after the arrival of the Tiffin family in Virginia, Edward resumed the course of medical studies he had begun in England, and in due time attended a course of lectures at the Jefferson Medical College of Pennsylvania and was licensed to practise. He was but twenty years of age, but had gained such reputation for learning and ability as to procure for him very quickly a remunerative business.

In 1789 he married Mary Worthington, daughter of Robert Worthington, of Berkeley County, and sister of Thomas Worthington, who afterward followed Tiffin in the office of Governor of Ohio, and preceded him in the office of senator from that State in the Congress of the United States.

This wife, with whom he lived most happily for nineteen years, was a beautiful and accomplished woman whose sweet fame for charity, piety, and dutifulness has come down to the present generation of the residents of southern Ohio as a cherished tradition. Of her, Bishop Asbury, of the M. E. Church, wrote: "She was one of the most conscientious and heavenly-minded women I have ever known." She died, childless, in 1808.

The year following his marriage, both Edward Tiffin and his wife were deeply impressed with religious feelings, evoked by the preaching of Rev. Thomas Scott (a young minister of the Methodist Episcopal persuasion; and who afterwards, as a successful lawyer and local preacher, lived neighbor and intimate friend to the Tiffins in Chillicothe for many years), and both publicly united with that branch of the Christian Church.

Tiffin was naturally quick, impulsive, energetic, and enthusiastic, and within a month after his union with the church, without a preparatory course of theological studies, without waiting for license or ordination to the ministry, he had gathered a large congregation of his associates and fellow-citizens of Berkeley County, and was fervently, eloquently, and effectively urging upon them the faith he had so recently embraced.

It was about two years after he had begun and continued to preach the Gospel of Jesus Christ that Bishop Asbury, in exercise of the powers vested in him by his office, ordained Edward Tiffin, on the nineteenth day of November, 1792, a deacon of the Methodist Episcopal Church, and so authorized him to preach. The fervency with which his religious life began never afterward abated in any degree; on the contrary, it steadily intensified through all his lifetime.

The parents of his wife having died prior to his marriage, he and his brother-in-law, Thomas Worthington, each became by inheritance the owner of sixteen negro slaves. The ownership of these negroes forced upon him the consideration of the humanity and morality of the institution of slavery; and neither the legality of it under the laws of the State of Virginia, the almost universal acceptance and approval of it by his fellow-citizens, nor the antiquity of its existence in this country and the world, could still the accusations of his sensitive conscience for partaking of its benefits to the master-class, or conceal from his clear perception the many iniquities which were necessarily and inherently connected with the system. His brother-in-law shared in all these thoughts and feelings, and the ultimate result of their many conferences upon the subject was that both resolved to manumit their slaves and remove to new homes within the territory northwest of the Ohio River, where the existence of slavery was prohibited forever by the provisions of the " Ordinance of 1787." This resolve, as soon as possible, both afterward carried into execution.

It is always interesting, when reading biographies, and especially so where portraiture is lacking, to catch glimpses of the personal appearance and manner of the subject of the sketch.

Edward Tiffin had now lived for fourteen years in Virginia, and from one who knew him intimately during those years I quote : " His natural buoyancy of spirits and vivacity, his sprightliness and pleasant manners, joined with unusual conversational powers, made him the favorite in the gay and fashionable circles of old Berkeley, and the very life and soul of whatever company he was in."

It was about the end of that period that George Washington, in a letter to Governor St. Clair (hereafter quoted in full), wrote of Tiffin that he possessed " a knowledge of law, resulting from close application " (to its study) " for a considerable time." Now, as those fourteen years were the years of his professional studies and largest medical practice, his gayest social life, his courtship and marriage, his conversion and the beginning of his ministry, and the period within which his study of politics (by which he became a very respectable statesman) must have been pursued—if he, also, in those years found time to obtain the knowledge of the science of law with which Washington credits him, Edward Tiffin must have been indeed a marvel of "sprightliness."

CHAPTER II

WE must now follow Edward Tiffin to his new home. The "Territory of the United States Northwest of the River Ohio," from which five great States were subsequently formed, had been earliest explored by civilized men, and occupied by military posts, by the French. In 1759 it had been wrested from the French by the English, and while the struggle was pending between England and her American colonies, known to us as the Revolutionary War, it was in turn wrested from the English by the Virginians, commanded by George Rodgers Clark, in a campaign scarcely paralleled for audacity of conception, skill in execution, pertinacious endurance of hardships, and heroic struggle against seeming hopelessness, in all the history of the world.

After the independence of the United States had been achieved, Virginia made this conquest by Clark the basis of a claim to sovereignty over the whole northwest; which title she afterward patriotically relinquished to the Federal Government in 1783, only reserving the fee of the lands lying between the Scioto and Little Miami rivers, to be devoted to satisfying the bounty land warrants she had issued to her citizens for military services during the Revolutionary War. But the whole of that area was inhabited by hostile Indians; and prior to 1795 no settlement was made by white people in what is now Ohio, save under the guardianship and protection of a military post and garrison of regular troops.

The crushing defeat of the confederated Indians by Anthony Wayne at Fallen Timbers, in 1794, followed by the treaty of Greenville in 1795, made it possible to settle, with comparative safety, other parts of the State with civilized people.

Nathaniel Massie, a very intelligent, brave, and enterprising young surveyor, had at great risk made various explorations and surveys in the Scioto Valley in 1793-94 and '95. In the early spring of 1796 he led a party of adventurous Virginians and Kentuckians up the Scioto, and laid out the present beautiful city of Chillicothe—the first successful location of a town outside of military protection ever made in Ohio, with the single exception of the stockaded post on the north bank of the Ohio River, in what is now Adams County,

originally known as Massie's Station, and now
known as the town of Manchester. This place,
also, had been established by Nathaniel Massie, in
1792, as a base for his surveying expeditions to
the north of the Ohio River.

Chillicothe being located within the reservation
thus made by Virginia, and in the heart of the wonderfully fertile and beautiful Scioto Valley, the new
town and the country around it at once stongly
attracted the attention and interest of Virginians,
and many of them sought homes there in the
years immediately following 1796; so that within
two years the town and country around it contained a population of nearly, or quite, one thousand souls. Of these Virginia emigrants there was
a party of sixteen or eighteen left Berkeley County
in the very early spring of 1798, and after thirty
days' travel reached the village of Chillicothe on
the twenty-seventh day of April. In this group
were Edward Tiffin and his wife, his parents, two
sisters, and two brothers; Thomas Worthington
and his wife; three or four white mechanics who
were employed by Worthington for the purpose
of building a mill; and several of the manumitted
negroes who, it was thought, could do better in
the new country than it was probable, or possible,
for them to do in Virginia.

Tiffin selected a four-acre lot on the northeast
corner of Water and High streets, and soon erected

upon it a large and commodious stone house which, except for brief periods afterward spent upon his farm in Union Township, and in Washington City, continued to be his residence until his death in 1829.

He immediately resumed the active practice of his profession, and as he was (so far as we can ascertain) at first the only medical practitioner in the rapidly growing settlement, and as the whole region was horribly malarious, as new and rich valleys of the West always are, he was compelled to ride on horseback night and day, far and wide. There were then, at best, only paths through the densely wooded wilderness, and no bridges over the many streams around Chillicothe, which were often swollen to deep, swift, and dangerous torrents. His life at that period was a busy and arduous one. It is traditionally said of him that he never refused his services because of weather or of distance to his patients, nor for the reason that a patient was too poor to compensate him for attendance. To anticipate a little, it is recorded of him by Mr. Williams that in his after years, and while occupied by duties of the highest official stations his fellow-citizens could bestow upon him—yea, even when the disease which terminated his life prevented him from leaving his own bed-chamber, it was his habit to receive, diagnose, and treat the poor, gratuitously, on set days of the week. "Indeed," says

Williams, "his benevolence to the poor and needy was bounded only by his ability to relieve them."

That he was competent and successful as a physician and surgeon many instances are given. One of these I quote from a paper written by his son-in-law, the late eminent and learned Dr. C. G. Comegys, of Cincinnati, Ohio: "Being upon one occasion distant from his home and without his surgical case, a terrible accident to a farmer in Union Township required that an immediate amputation of a leg should be performed. Dr. Tiffin quickly improvised all the instruments necessary for the operation, performed it skillfully and successfully and saved his patient's life."

I have stated that the entire Tiffin family came to Ohio together. These were his father, Henry Tiffin, who died in 1807; his mother, who survived her husband some years, dying in 1810; the oldest brother, Henry; his sister Mary, who married Captain Isaac Davis; Joseph, who married Nancy Dorsey Wood, of Maryland *; and Margaret, who married John Gardiner, long an associate judge of Common Pleas for Ross County. The brothers and sisters each left several children, and their descendants are now numerous and widely scattered throughout the United States.

---

* This couple were the grandparents of the author of this memoir.

CHAPTER III

WHILE Edward Tiffin lived in Virginia he seems to have imbibed the intense interest in political affairs and the desire to hold public office which is so generally characteristic of the inhabitants of that State.

In 1798 Major-General Arthur St. Clair was governor of the United States Territory Northwest of the Ohio River. He had been appointed to that office October 5, 1787, and had removed to the Territory and assumed the duties of his office as early as July 9, 1788, a few months after the first permanent settlement by white people in Ohio—that of the Ohio Land Company at Marietta, which occurred in April, 1788.

St. Clair was born a British subject at Caithness, Scotland, in 1734. His family was one which had

high social and political rank in Scotland, and has
frequent mention in Scottish history and poetry.
He was possessed of excellent intellectual endow-
ments, was well educated, and polished by inter-
course with the best civil and military society.
He had held a royal commission as captain in the
British army, and distinguished himself by gallan-
try at the capture of Quebec.   In 1760 he married
Miss Phœbe Bayard, of Boston, Mass., and in 1762
he resigned his commission in the British army.
He had been a member of the Continental Congress, and a president of that body.   In December,
1775, he was commissioned by John Hancock a
colonel of the Colonial army.   He served through
the Revolutionary War as an American officer, and
attained the rank of a major-general.   Unquestion-
ably he had become thoroughly Americanized and
devoted to the interests of his adopted country.
But unfortunately he was proud, aristocratic, arbitrary and stubborn, and consequently became un-
popular, especially with the Virginians, when that
class began to fill up the reservation.   Subsequent events, and especially the course the governor pursued toward the Territorial Legislature
when it met, rapidly deepened and widened the
chasm between St. Clair and the Virginians; and
the latter found some sympathizers and allies
among the New England settlers, and particularly
among the New Jersey settlers who came to the

John Cleve Symmes' purchase in the Miami country.

As between St. Clair and the leaders of "the Virginia party" living in Chillicothe, we shall see that the quarrel soon grew to be "war, war to the knife, and the knife to the hilt."

In such conditions it was to be expected that much unwarranted abuse and misrepresentation would be heaped upon St. Clair's head, and it came to be often asserted, and very generally believed in southwestern portions of the Territory, that he was at heart disloyal to American theories of government by the people and in favor of an hereditary monarchy. This was not only utterly untrue of him; it was cruel and ungrateful.*

Dr. Tiffin brought with him from Virginia a letter written by George Washington and addressed to Governor St. Clair, which we copy in full because it constitutes a high tribute to the character of Tiffin from the very highest source in the world at the time, and is, so far as the author of this sketch is aware, the only letter of recommendation of an aspirant for official appoint-

---

* Tardy justice, in part at least, has been done to the character, reputation, and patriotic services of St. Clair by the recent publication of his *Papers*, under an order and appropriation by the General Assembly of Ohio. They have been ably edited by William Henry Smith, of Chicago, Ill., and published by Robert Clark & Co., of Cincinnati, Ohio, 1882.

ment ever written by Washington in behalf of any person :—

"*January 4th*, 1798.

"*Sir:*—Mr. Edward Tiffin solicits an appointment in the territory Northwest of the Ohio.

" The fairness of his character in private and public life, together with a knowledge of law, resulting from close application for a considerable time, will, I hope, justify the liberty I now take in recommending him to your attention. Regarding with due attention the delicacy as well as the importance of the character in which I act, I am sure you will do me the justice to believe that nothing but the knowledge of the gentleman's merits, founded upon a long acquaintance, could have induced me to trouble you on this occasion.

" With sincere wishes for your happiness and welfare, I am, etc., etc.

"GEO. WASHINGTON."

That this letter was duly delivered to St. Clair is evident from the fact that it has been until lately in the custody of Dr. W. H. St. Clair, of Effingham County, Ill.—Dr. St. Clair being a great-grandson of General Arthur St. Clair, to whom it was addressed. It is now in the State archives at Columbus, Ohio. Whether it bore fruit by securing an office for Dr. Tiffin does not certainly appear; but the doctor was, within three or four months after his arrival in the Territory, appointed and commissioned prothonotary for Ross County, and his name appears, subscribed as such official, to the records of the first session of the first Territorial Court of Common Pleas, held "in and for the county of Ross," in December, 1798, and in many successive terms thereafter. He continued to hold the office of prothonotary and discharge all its duties until the beginning of the January term, 1803, notwithstanding that he, in the meantime, also continued the active practice of medicine, and to gather, organize, and regularly minister to Methodist Episcopal societies in all the surrounding country; and in the fall of 1799 successfully canvassed for election to the first Territorial legislature.

Indeed, the lines of his active employments were so numerous in these three or four years that it is difficult to tell the story of them connectedly and satisfactorily. Beside all else, he had been Speaker of the House of Representatives, President of the Ohio Constitutional Convention, and was the Governor-elect of Ohio before he ceased to be prothonotary of Common Pleas!

That Washington was correct in estimating him to possess a considerable knowledge of law is apparent from an examination of his records and

2

memoranda of those early terms of the court. They prove that Tiffin was better versed in the artificial and involved forms of the old practice at common law than were most of the lawyers, and some of the judges, of that day.

CHAPTER IV

The Territory attains the Necessary Population for a Legislature—Tiffin elected a Delegate—Character of First
General Assembly—Tiffin elected Speaker—Opposition
to St. Clair develops—County Seat Controversy—St.
Clair's Many Vetoes—Harrison defeats St. Clair's Son
for Congress—Byrd appointed Territorial Secretary—
His Animosity to the Governor—Territory of Indiana
created—Opposition to St. Clair's Reappointment—St.
Clair suddenly dissolves General Assembly—His Reappointment as Governor.

THE reader must bear in mind that when Governor St. Clair caused a census to be taken of the
Territory Northwest of the Ohio River in 1798,
that Territory was yet in its entirety, as it was at
the time of the adoption of the Ordinance of 1787.
That it was found by this census to contain five
thousand free white male inhabitants over the age
of twenty-one years within its boundaries, therefore,
means there was then that number of such inhabitants within the vast area which now constitutes the
States of Ohio, Michigan, Indiana, Illinois, Wiscon-
sin, and a part of Minnesota ; in other words, all
the country belonging to the United States which

lay to the north of the Ohio River and east of the Mississippi River.

In obedience to the mandate of the ordinance, St. Clair ordered an election of delegates to the first Territorial legislature, and on the third Monday of December, 1798, the election took place accordingly. Edward Tiffin was one of those chosen, and his colleagues from Ross County were Thomas Worthington, Samuel Findley and Major Elias Langham. Of the body of men chosen to constitute this first legislature of the Northwest, almost every individual was a man of marked characteristics, and many of them of such intellectual powers and educational acquirements as would surely elevate them to distinction and leadership were they living members of the United States Congress in this last quarter of the nine. teenth century. I therefore name some of those who represented the parts of the Territory which are now included within the State of Ohio. Besides the delegates already named from Ross County there were:

From Hamilton County, Robert Benham, afterward a distinguished lawyer and orator; William McMillen, afterward a delegate to Congress; John Smith, afterward a senator of the United States; Dr. William Goforth, afterward a member of the Constitutional Convention, and distinguished for attainments in the natural sciences.

From Adams County, Nathaniel Massie, the pioneer surveyor and founder of Chillicothe, a member of the Constitutional Convention, and candidate for governor of the State in 1807.

From Washington County, Return Jonathan Meigs, Jr., afterward a justice of the Supreme Court of Ohio, governor of the State of Ohio, senator of the United States, and postmaster-general of the United States; and Paul Fearing, afterward a delegate to Congress.

These names indicate the class of people who settled the Northwest and whose descendants now largely predominate in it; and this explains the fact, now so commonly known and admitted as to be proverbial, that "the Ohio man" is a political force and power in this country which cannot be ignored.

This legislature was ordered by the proclamation to meet at Cincinnati on the 22d of January 1799, for the purpose of naming to the President of the United States ten residents of the Territory, from whom the President was to select five to form a "Legislative Council," a body corresponding to the Senate of our present State General Assembly.

When it is remembered that the delegates were compelled to travel by horseback through the wilderness, some of them from Kaskaski on the Mississippi, and from Vincennes on the Wabash, and Detroit in the peninsula of Michigan, and similar great distances, it is not surprising that it was as late as the 4th of February before a quorum had convened. When it did assemble they attempted no permanent organization, but simply selected the ten names and transmitted them to President Adams (from which list he afterward selected Robert Oliver of Washington County, Jacob Burnet and James Finley of Hamilton County, Henry Vanderburgh of Knox, and David Vance of Jefferson, to constitute the council), and adjourned to meet again at Cincinnati on the sixteenth day of the following September.

Again the same causes worked delay, and it was not until the 23d of that month that a quorum was secured and an organization effected. Edward Tiffin was unanimously elected speaker.

Here is a proper place to refute an often repeated slander upon the early settlers of the Territory, and especially the Virginia and Kentucky contingent of them; to wit: that they desired to fasten the institution of domestic slavery upon the Northwest.

A petition was presented to that first legislature at its first session, from certain persons still resident in Virginia, who were holders of land warrants which were entitled to location in the military reservation, for permission to settle upon their locations and retain their negro slaves in bondage. That petition was not even considered;

the sixth clause of the Ordinance of 1787, in the opinion of all the delegates, made it impossible to grant such permission. And we are told by Judge Jacob Burnet, himself a distinguished member of the Legislative Council, that " such was the feeling and temper of the delegates in regard to the system of human slavery, that *if there had been no such prohibition in the ordinance, the request would have been refused, as it was, by a unanimous vote.*" " The members," continues Judge Burnet in his *Notes,* " were not only opposed to slavery on the ground of its being a moral evil, in violation of human rights, but they were of the opinion that it would retard the settlement of the territory by making labor less reputable, and by cultivating habits and feelings unfriendly to the simplicity and industry they desired to encourage and perpetuate."

But to return to our more immediate subject. Notwithstanding the session seemed to open under fair auspices, with complimentary addresses and much good advice from the governor, and pleasant responses and promises by President Vanderburgh, of the Legislative Council, and Speaker Tiffin, that St. Clair's suggestions should be carefully heeded, all knew that a storm was brewing which would inevitably burst upon the governor's head sooner or later.

As early as 1788—the first year of his administration—St. Clair had clashed with Judges Sargent

and Varnum. Acting under a provision of the
ordinance which directed that " the governor and
judges, *or a majority of them,* shall adopt such laws
of the original States, civil and criminal, as may
be necessary," etc., Sargent and Varnum, judges,
differed from St. Clair, governor, as to what should
be adopted. St. Clair contended that by virtue of
his office of governor his assent was necessary to
the adoption of any law, and so controlled the
majority of the council. Thus early he asserted
his autocratic nature, although in this instance he
yielded his opinion. He had created much dis-
satisfaction by claiming the fees for marriage
licenses, ferry licenses and tavern licenses, as
official perquisites to himself. But he created the
most excitement and opposition by contending
for the sole power to locate county seats. This
controversy began in 1798, after Adams County
had been created. Nathaniel Massie had laid out
the town of Manchester and naturally desired that
it should be the county seat, and the judges and
justices of the new county coincided with him.
The governor ordered that Adamsville should be
chosen, and forbade the local magistrates from
proceeding to erect the courthouse and jail at
Manchester, and ordered the treasurer to pay out
no moneys upon account of such buildings.

The legislature took up the subject and held
that it was now vested with power both to create

new counties and to fix the county seats. They selected Manchester, but the bill was vetoed by the governor. In this controversy Massie led the opposition to the governor, and he had the zealous support of all the Virginians.

This General Assembly at its first session passed thirty-nine bills, and Governor St. Clair vetoed eleven of them.

President Adams had appointed William Henry Harrison secretary of the Territory, shortly before this session of the Territorial Assembly, to succeed Winthrop Sargent, who had been promoted to the office of Governor of Mississippi Territory. This was a most unwelcome appointment to St. Clair. His biographer says, " Between St. Clair and the new secretary there was no bond of sympathy." Probably because there was no such bond, this legislature elected William H. Harrison the Territorial delegate to Congress over Arthur St. Clair, Jr., the governor's son, by a vote of eleven to ten. Harrison hastened to take his seat in Congress, and his work adverse to St. Clair soon became evident.

The vacant secretaryship of the Territory was now filled by the appointment by the President, on December 30, 1799, of Charles Willing Byrd. If there was no bond of sympathy between St. Clair and Harrison, there was positive repulsion between the governor and Byrd, whose selection was due to the influences exerted by Harrison and

Thomas Worthington, who were then in Philadelphia, as St. Clair shrewdly suspected, laboring to secure such a division of the Territory as the Virginians desired, viz.: by a line run due north from the mouth of the Great Miami; and to defeat the scheme of St. Clair to have it divided by a line run due north from Eagle Creek, which would, the governor thought, indefinitely postpone the formation of a State from the eastern part of it by reason of the lack of sufficient population.

The act of Congress passed in May, 1800, created the Territory of Indiana out of the western part of the "Territory Northwest of the Ohio River," the dividing line being drawn due north from the mouth of the Great Miami. The eastern portion retained the original name. The same act designated Chillicothe as the seat of government for the latter Territory. This was a great victory for the Virginia party, and a corresponding mortification to St. Clair and his adherents.

The second session of this first General Assembly was, therefore, held in Chillicothe. It convened on the 5th day of November, 1800, and was again opened by an address from the governor which culminated in bitter denunciations of his political enemies. Both branches of the Assembly, through their respective presiding officers, replied to the governor's address in good temper, with respectful and conciliatory words; but nevertheless the antagonism went on, more manifest, however, outside the halls of the legislature than within them.

It was known, of course, that St. Clair's term as governor of the Territory expired by limitation on the 9th of December of that year, and active measures were employed to prevent his reappointment by the President. In the meantime St. Clair had prepared a "*coup*" for the Assembly, which had no idea of concluding its session so soon. On the 2d of December he suddenly informed them that their session must terminate on the 9th inst., with the ending of his term as governor.

Judge Burnet, a warm friend of St. Clair, in his *Notes* thus speaks of this piece of strategy:

"It is remarkable that the governor concealed his purpose to adjourn the legislature until it was too late to confer with the secretary of the Territory, who was then absent from the seat of government, as it was known that his (the secretary's) opinion of his powers coincided with that of the legislature, and it was not doubted that if such conference were had he (the secretary) would have taken the responsibility of issuing his proclamation at once, bearing date next day after the termination of the governor's term of office, reassembling the two houses forthwith, before the members should separate and return to their respective homes. By that means the sitting of the Assembly would have been continued until the public business then pending was disposed of."

The efforts to prevent the reappointment of St. Clair to the governorship of the Territory failed, for on the 22d day of December, 1800, President Adams sent his nomination to the Senate, where, after a brief struggle, it was duly confirmed on the 3d of February, 1801, and St. Clair seemed to have won the decisive and permanent victory over his political enemies. But an event of evil portent to him soon occurred. On the 4th day of March, 1801, Thomas Jefferson was inaugurated President of the United States, and the Virginians in the Territory hailed the event with joy and hope. Yet, as will appear, they were destined to feel something of the heart-sickness which comes of " hope deferred."

CHAPTER V

IN October, 1801, the election of members for the second Territorial General Assembly occurred, and a number of changes were made in the *personnel* of the house. Ross County reëlected Tiffin, Worthington, Findley, and Langham. When this Assembly convened at Chillicothe on the 24th of November, 1801, Edward Tiffin was again unanimously chosen as speaker. When it is remembered that St. Clair had many devoted partisans in this house, and that Tiffin was most prominent among those in opposition to him and his policies, this unanimity is most remarkable, and seems to be a high testimonial to Tiffin's personal character, and to his ability and fairness in administration of the speakership.

And he was still prothonotary of Ross County Common Pleas and clerk of the Supreme Court; he was still practising medicine " between times " ; he was still gathering Methodist societies together, and preaching to one or another of them almost every Sabbath day!

It is not my purpose to follow the details of the transactions of this General Assembly further than to state that, a vacancy having occurred in the Territorial representation in Congress, by the appointment of William Henry Harrison to be governor of the new Territory of Indiana, William McMillen, of Hamilton County, was chosen to fill the balance of his unexpired term, and Paul Fearing, of Washington, the full term to follow. Both of these gentlemen were especial friends and partisans of St. Clair, and St. Clair had sufficient influence with the members to get a majority of them to assent to a proposition to re-divide the Territory in such a way as, St. Clair thought, would prevent the formation of a State out of any portion of it for many years to come ; and also to remove the sittings of the Assembly from Chillicothe to Cincinnati again.

To develop fully the personal character and the public services of Edward Tiffin, it will now be necessary to return to 1798 and bring up the history of the development of political parties in the Territory, and also the story of the eager and ardent contest, partly political, which culminated in the organization of the State of Ohio.

The earliest pioneers — those who came to Marietta and Cincinnati in 1788 and the immediately succeeding years — brought no political quarrels with them. Governor St. Clair was the first individual in all the Northwest Territory of whom we hear as a political partisan, and for ten years the only one. His admiring biographer, William Henry Smith, says "he was an ardent Federalist." He desired in 1792 to resign the governorship of the Territory and accept from the Federalists the place of member of Congress from the Westmoreland district in Pennsylvania. His letters to his intimate friend, Senator James Ross, of Pennsylvania (in whose honor he had named Ross County, in the Territory), are full of strong expressions of his hatred of Thomas Jefferson's principles and partisans; he characterized the Democratic-Republican party as "the damned faction that was dragging the country to ruin." He wrote and published a pamphlet in defence and support of "the Alien and Sedition Laws," and sent a copy to President John Adams, and, in short, constantly and prominently displayed zeal as a Federalist political partisan. The Virginians and Kentuckians who came to the reservation with Massie in 1796, and to the Scioto Valley in the two or three following years, soon became unfriendly to St. Clair, it is true ; but their hostility grew out of his administration of Territorial affairs, and not at all, *at first* at least, because of his opinions upon national politics.

The very earliest hint of the formation of a national Democratic-Republican party in the Territory was the refusal of Shadrach Bond, William Goforth, Elias Langham, John Ludlow, and Return Jonathan Meigs, Jr., to vote for an adulatory address to President Adams, adopted at the close of the first General Assembly. It is to be noted that this list contains the name of only one Virginian, Mr. Langham. Speaker Tiffin, Worthington, Massie, Findley, Darlinton, and all the rest of the anti-St. Clair members supported it with apparent cordiality.

But very early in 1799 the idea of forming a State immediately, out of the eastern part of the Territory Northwest of the Ohio, began to be mooted publicly. It had been privately discussed and resolved upon months before by the leaders of the anti-St. Clair faction, and St. Clair was well aware of the design, and manœuvred diligently and skilfully to defeat it. After President Adams had reappointed St. Clair to office, despite all their efforts to prevent it, the Virginians and Kentuckians in the Territory, and a considerable contingent of the settlers from other States, turned to Jefferson and his party—whose early success they anticipated—and courted their favor and assistance. That Jefferson was a Virginian made this easy for them to do; and that most of the enemies of St. Clair were Virginians inclined Jefferson to aid them. That St. Clair himself was an avowed, radical, and active Federalist probably concluded the determination of the future President as to his line of conduct in the premises, after inauguration.

Worthington and the brilliant but dissipated Michael Baldwin had been sent by the State party to Philadelphia, to labor with the President and Congress in behalf of the State project, while Tiffin and Massie and William Creighton, Jr., vigilantly watched and aggressively assaulted the forces of St. Clair in the West.

It is almost pathetic to know that when the Federalists of the Territory wished to send Judge Tod, of Trumbull County, and William McMillen, of Hamilton County, to Philadelphia to counteract the work of Worthington and Baldwin, they were prevented from carrying out the purpose by their inability to raise the money necessary to defray the expenses of their two agents, which St. Clair and Judge Tod estimated at about three hundred dollars! Nevertheless they seemed still to have the advantages all in their favor. The second General Assembly had declared against assuming immediate statehood, and consented to a further division of the Territory by the line of the Scioto River. A mass meeting of the citizens of Marietta had passed

3

—with only Return Jonathan Meigs, his son, and a very few others dissenting—resolutions strongly denouncing the project; and they had issued an address to the inhabitants of the Territory, giving plausible reasons why the territorial condition was best for their interests for some years to come, at least.   William McMillen, a decided anti-State man, had, in May, 1800, succeeded Harrison (who at that time became governor of the new Territory of Indiana) as delegate to Congress; and St. Clair had stanch friends in both the Senate and House of Representatives, notably the Pennsylvania senator, James Ross.

All through the years of 1800 and 1801 the two or three newspapers of the Territory teemed with articles *pro et con;* those favoring the State formation coming from the pens of Tiffin, Worthington, Creighton and Massie, and those *contra* written by St. Clair, Judge Burnet, Solomon Sibley and Charles Hammond—the latter a very able young man, destined in later years to become distinguished among the intellectual men of Ohio.   Judge Jacob Burnet, a decided Federalist and warm friend of St. Clair's, as already stated, admits in his *Notes on the Early Settlement of the Northwest* (pp. 378–381) that, "as the discussion went on, St. Clair's supporters fast deserted him, and before it closed, a majority of his friends and admirers were politically associated with his most active opponents."   " In the long struggle," says William Henry Smith, the biographer of St. Clair, " Dr. Tiffin seems to have been the most determined and active advocate of State organization, and was the spur to the energies of Massie, Worthington, Creighton and others."

It is notable, too, that the discussion of this question was seldom broached in the legislative halls, and when it was, it was only by the anti-State party. The State party labored hard to create favorable public opinion in the Territory, it is true, but it seems to have been their policy to work upon the President and Congress for effective results. They fully realized that their proposition could not obtain a majority of votes either in the General Assembly or from the people of the Territory for a long while to come, and they carefully avoided permitting an expression upon it from either, whenever it was possible to avoid it.

I had hoped to embody here, in this memoir, a copy of an address to the inhabitants of the Territory, written by Dr. Tiffin and published in the *Scioto Gazette*, October, 1801, as an answer to the Marietta address to which I have alluded, for the double purpose of giving my readers the best statement of the argument in favor of the immediate formation of a State which was published during the controversy, and of furnishing a good specimen of Tiffin's style of composition and power in argumentation ; but unfortunately the article is lost and cannot be replaced further than to copy such extracts from it as were quoted by William Henry Smith in his *St. Clair Papers* (vol. i., pp. 225–227).

Mr. Smith says: " It was the most reasonable statement of that side of the case, and painted the future " (of such State if formed) " in bright colors."

Tiffin argued that " a territorial government was ill-adapted to the genius and feelings of Americans "; that it was " only necessary to direct attention to the Ordinance of Congress for the government of the Territory, to convince one of the utter impossibility of a government conducive to national happiness in this enlightened day being administrated under it, unless by persons more than mortal. It was formulated at a time when civil liberty was not so fully understood as it is now, and contemplated only a government by the few over the many. . . .

" It is said by the remonstrants [in the Marietta address] that no community ought to wish to emerge from this territorial condition, unless there be danger that the paramount government will infringe upon its rights, until that community has made comfortable provision for its expenses; until it has made considerable progress in its improvements in agricultural development; until it has made arrangements for the education of its people; until it has consolidated its social system; in short, until it has not only become fully able to bear the

weight of its own independence, but also to preserve its liberties and principles by force. It is
then asked by the remonstrants, ' Is this our situation ? Where are our improvements? What the
state of our agriculture? Of our commerce? Of
our manufactories?' etc., etc., etc. To all of which
I answer, that in my opinion a State government
offers the only probable way to secure these desir-
able conditions. To talk about our liberties being
infringed upon by the paramount government,
when we have no liberties in our present state,
is like the moral to the fable which concludes
the Marietta address—it is all sound ; no substance. . . .

"We entered upon the second grade of this
territorial government much in debt and without
a cent in the treasury. We had recourse to paper.
This present year's revenue will redeem all our
paper and furnish cash for the current year's expenses. . . .

" Much progress has been made in the improvement of our lands, and provisions for education ;
but they cannot be perfected under present conditions. It is well known to you that men of wealth
and sentiments of independence are deterred from
migrating to this Territory because they cannot
brook to live under our present government.

" But let the change come, let a government con-
genial to American sentiments be adopted, and it

will be like opening the flood-gates to a mill!
Wealth will flow in upon us; improvements will
adorn our lands; agriculture will flourish; our
rivers emptying into the Ohio will convey, by way
of the Mississippi, our surplus crops to thousands
suffering from want of food. Manufactories will
spring up in this wilderness; arrangements and
facilities for education will be perfected; an Athens
and other centers of learning will show steeples
above our towering oaks, and soon send our youth
into the world, ornaments to humanity. Our plains
will be covered with herds; our farms, laden from
the horn of plenty, will gladden our farmers' hearts;
and our government, like a tree of liberty, will extend its shelter over all our citizens and cause all
men to contemplate our rising greatness with
amazement, and our people to cry out with the
venerable Franklin, 'Here dwells Liberty! Here
is *my* Country!'"

In the absence of the full text of the foregoing,
I here insert the summary of the contention of
the State party as given by Judge Burnet in his
Notes:

"It was alleged" (by the State party) "that the
existing government was anti-republican; that the
inhabitants of the Territory did not enjoy the
political rights which belonged to freemen; that

neither the governor, the judges of the General Court, nor the Legislative Council were in any form amenable to the people; that the power of appointing to office, exercised by Congress, was a dangerous one and had been abused; that the governor controlled the will of the representatives of the people, and that there was no remedy for these evils save by a radical change of government."

CHAPTER VI

JEFFERSON had now occupied the presidential chair for some months, while the efforts of the State party had been pressed unremittingly, not only for the creation of the State, but also for the removal of St. Clair.

Worthington had remained, most of the time, at the seat of national government, where he had brought all possible influences to bear to accomplish both these purposes. He made very evident progress in the matter of securing statehood, but in dislodging St. Clair from his position (scarcely less desired by him and his circle of immediate friends) his progress was not obvious. He had secured the very active and zealous support of William B. Giles, an able, influential and exceedingly energetic member of Congress from Virginia, and to a great extent the favor and support of the Republican Democrats in both Senate and House (and that party was in the ascendant in Congress then) to the proposition to form a State from the eastern part of the Northwest Territory. And no doubt—indeed it is certain—the President quietly and privately assumed the guidance of the State project through his friend and partisan, Giles; for, would it not most probably strengthen his party, and secure to himself three more electoral votes? (he had attained the presidency only by choice of the House of Representatives, after a tie in the electoral college) as well as three more zealous friends on the floors of Congress? But in the matter of removing General St. Clair the President *seemed*, at least, loath to act. Let us hope that he thought of St. Clair's services as a soldier in the War for Independence, and his patriotic devotion and zeal as a member of the old Congress in the formative days of the United States Government, and therefore hesitated to inflict the blow, notwithstanding St. Clair's Federalism.

Formal charges of the maladministration of his office, and personal misconduct which amounted to "high crimes and misdemeanors," had been drawn up by Massie against Governor St. Clair upon the urgency of Worthington and Tiffin, and with the assistance of Tiffin, and were by Worthington filed with the President on the 30th of February, 1802, accompanied by a very strong and bitter personal letter reciting the proofs which, Worthington thought, fully sustained the charges. That Tiffin took a willing and an eager part in getting up these charges against Governor St. Clair, sufficiently appears in the following extracts from letters written by him to Worthington.

Under date of February 1, 1802, he says:

"I have used every exertion to get Colonel Massie to draw up and forward his charges. We have appointed three different times to meet on that business, and I have always attended but could never get him there. He has now left town, and when I shall see him again, I know not."

And again, under date of February 8th, he wrote:

"We have this day been busy in drawing up charges to forward to the Secretary of State against Governor St. Clair. Colonel Massie, Mr. Creighton and myself meet again at my house on Wednesday. We will send them on by the next mail thereafter, most certainly."

And on the 20th he wrote:

"I expect ere this you have received the charges against the Governor; I had much trouble to get Colonel Massie to finish them."

Whether this participation in this business was creditable or otherwise to Edward Tiffin, I leave the reader to judge ; perhaps the exigencies of the political situation at the time justified it.

These charges were as follows :

" 1. He (Governor St. Clair) has usurped legislative powers by the erection of courts and location of the seats of justice, by proclamation, on his own sole authority.

" 2. He has misused the power of negativing legislative acts, by putting his negative against laws useful and necessary for the Territory.

" 3. He has refused to perform the duties of his office except on the payment of arbitrary fees not established by any lawful authority.

" 4. He has negatived acts of the Legislature abolishing those fees, and approved an act giving him $500 which was meant as a compensation for that abolition—thereby holding both the fees and the compensation for them.

" 5. He has attempted to affect the dismemberment of the Territory, and to destroy its constitutional boundaries, in order to prevent its advancement to those rights of self-government to which its numbers [of inhabitants] would entitle it.

" 6. He has granted commissions generally during [his] pleasure ; but that of Attorney-General to his own son, during good behavior.

" 7. He has endeavored arbitrarily to influence and control the proceedings of the judiciary, and has revoked or effected the surrender of the commissions of those who have refused to bend to his will.

" 8. He has appointed persons residing out of a county to offices, the duties of which were to be habitually performed within them.

" 9. He has neglected, and thereby obstructed, the organization and discipline of a militia for the defense of the Territory, by withholding the appointment of officers for eighteen months after a law had passed establishing them.

" 10. He has avowed his hostility to the form and substance of republican government."

Upon these charges, greatly to the disappointment of the " Virginia Junto" (as they were habitually called by the Federalists), President Jefferson took no action. Indeed, we can nowhere find that he ever expressed any opinion whatever in regard to them.

But as, in the meantime, the project to create a State out of the eastern part of the Territory was rapidly going on to consummation, under the immediate guidance of the President it is believed, it is probable that Jefferson saw a way to dispose of St. Clair with less of public excitement and scandal than would be sure to ensue were he to remove him from office upon these charges.

The proposition of St. Clair to further divide the Territory of the Northwest by the line of the Scioto River, and thereby reduce the population of the eastern part to such a degree as to necessarily postpone its admission to statehood for a long time, had been approved, as we have seen, by the second General Assembly of the Territory ; it was now submitted to Congress by Mr. Fearing, the Federalist delegate from the Territory, for consideration and action. This strategical device of St. Clair's proved a veritable boomerang to him and his partisans, for it brought 'to the consideration of Congress the whole subject of the affairs of the Territory, and furnished the opportunity so ardently sought by the " Junto," whose greatest difficulty had been to get their projects up for action by Congress. The friends of St. Clair—the Federalists in Congress— had now furnished the opportunity, and by " lining up " in support of the propositions of St. Clair, had done much to array the whole strength of Jefferson's party against them.

Rev. Menassah Cutler, then a member of Congress, wrote to his son, Judge Ephraim Cutler of Marietta, under the date of February 1, 1802 :

" The law of your Territory providing for a dividing line has met with a spirited resistance and op-

position from Giles *and the whole of the reigning
majority.* Large budgets of petitions and other
documents have been laid by this Virginia leader
before the House. Mr. Fearing has acted his part
well, and has been supported generally by the
Federalists; but the subject is exceedingly unpop-
ular." . . . "The current of opposition to
the measure was so strong as to render it impossible to do anything to counteract it.

"Giles has brought forward a motion, the object
of which is to encourage and urge the people (*i.e.*,
the inhabitants of the Northwestern Territory) to
immediately become a State. This motion has
been referred to a committee which has not yet
reported."

The proposition to divide the Territory according to the request of the Territorial Assembly was,
after debate, rejected by the House on January 27,
1802, by the very decisive vote of eighty-one to
five, both Republicans and a majority of the Federalists voting against it.

Mr. Giles immediately followed up this advantage with the motion to which Mr. Cutler referred
in the quotation just made. On the 30th of March
the select committee to which it was referred made
their report to the committee of the whole House,
in which they not only recommended that an act
be passed—

" Enabling the inhabitants of the eastern division of the Territory Northwest of the Ohio River to form for themselves a constitution and state government," but also " for the *admission* of such state, when the government thereof shall be formed, into the Union upon the same footing with the original states, in all respects whatever, by the name of the State of ———." (The name was left blank.)

The committee also recommended that in such Enabling Act the northern boundary of the new State—

" Should be an east and west line drawn through the southerly extreme of Lake Michigan, running east after intersecting the due north line aforesaid from the mouth of the Great Miami" (*i.e.*, the western boundary line of the new State) "until it shall intersect Lake Erie or the territorial line ; and thence with the same through Lake Erie to the Pennsylvania line." *

It will be observed that this northern boundary line cut off from the then Territory of the Northwest, the county of Wayne, which included all of the peninsular part of what is now the State of

---

* The vague knowledge existing at that time of the geography of the lake region, and the clumsiness of the description of this northern boundary line, came near involving Ohio and Michigan in hostilities, about thirty years later.

Michigan. Judge Sibley undoubtedly gives, in a
letter, the true reason for that action. The inhabitants of Wayne County were nearly unanimously
opposed to the State party, and might defeat the
project if it became necessary to thereafter submit
it to a vote of the inhabitants of the Territory;
therefore its four or five thousand population was
set outside the area of the proposed State.

The report of the committee recites the section
of the Ordinance of 1787 which required sixty
thousand free inhabitants in any part of the Territory seeking to be erected into a State, and the
qualifying clause that " if consistent with the general interests of the Confederacy, such admission
shall be allowed at an earlier period and with a less
number of free inhabitants in any State than sixty
thousand"; and proceeds to argue that, although
the census taken more than twelve months before
showed only forty-five thousand three hundred and
sixty-five such inhabitants within the Territory
(from which number was to be deducted the three
thousand four hundred inhabitants of Wayne
County), yet from the rapid growth in population of
that section, as shown by the sale of five hundred
and fifty-three thousand nine hundred and ninety-
five acres of land in the eastern division since that
census was taken, it was probable that before all
the measures necessary for the formation of a constitution and putting into operation a State gov-

ernment could be accomplished, the number of inhabitants of the proposed State would reach sixty thousand; and therefore the 4th resolution of their report recommended:

" That until the next general census shall be taken, the State of ———— shall be entitled to ———— representatives in the House of Representatives of the United States."

Verily, exceptionally clear heads and very strong and unscrupulous hands guided the State movement; and we believe that one of those heads and a pair of those hands belonged to the body of Thomas Jefferson !

It was upon this report that the battle was fought out in Congress which decided the fate of the State project. Many speeches were made in support of and against its recommendations; the principal ones in support of the report being made by Giles of Virginia, Davis of Kentucky, Nicholson of Maryland, R. Williams of North Carolina, Goddard of Connecticut, and Macon of North Carolina. The principal arguments against the adoption of its recommendations were made by Paul Fearing, the territorial delegate, and Griswold of Connecticut. Although Rev. Menassah Cutler was a member of the House of Representatives at the time, and present in the chamber, and voted constantly

4

adversely to the State project, he made no speech
in support of his views.

Every objection to the report of the committee
having been voted down, it was agreed to on the
31st of March, and a bill in conformity to its recommendations ordered.   No wonder that Paul
Fearing about this time wrote to his friend Ephraim
Cutler :

" I presume you are tired of this business by this
time, and if you are not, I can tell you that I am
and have been for a long time.   My constant
prayer to God is, that in His goodness and power
—for some superior power is necessary—He will
confuse their councils and avert the evils which I
fear await us."

Edward Tiffin, although a preacher, did not shift
all responsibility for results upon God.   During all
this critical period he, with Massie, Creighton, and
doubtless others of whom we do not hear, were
wonderfully energetic and active in obtaining
signers from all parts of the Territory which were
to form the State, to petitions in favor of statehood,
and forwarding them to Worthington, who placed
them "where they would do the most good."   On
the 18th of January, Tiffin wrote to Worthington
that petitions, numerously signed, had been forwarded to him; and afterward he repeated the

notice of the going forward of many other petitions of a similar tenor. Mr. Giles, when speaking against the proposition to divide the Territory by the Scioto line, as early as January 20th said : " I have in my hands petitions signed by above a thousand of the inhabitants of that Territory against this proposed division."

It is a matter of surprise to us that the Anti-State party did not, to any considerable extent at least, avail themselves of the agency of petitions (the most direct means of reaching Congress) to aid their cause. We read of many protests being filed against the removal of St. Clair from the governorship, but of almost none at all against the formation of the State, although it is certain that, at first at least, a large majority of the people of the Territory were opposed to the change of government. This fact furnished the champions of the State party in the House of Representatives with their strongest argument. Mr. Nicholson of Kentucky, replying to the speech of Griswold of Connecticut (who had pointed out that no demand for State organization had come to Congress from any *legal* authority of the Territory), said :

" If the government of the territory remains as now organized, I believe we may wait till doomsday for their approbation. Have we not seen a law passed by that Legislature . . . for divid ing the territory in such manner as to defer their admission into the Union, and so enable the present governor and Legislative Council to hold their offices even after the territory, by reason of having sixty thousand population, had the *right* (under the Ordinance of 1787) to become a State? . . .

"The people of the territory, to the number of several thousands, have expressed the wish to be admitted into the Union. Who makes objection? It is only the delegate from the territory! Yes, he is the only man in the whole territory that opposes the wishes of the whole people of the territory!"

Hon. R. Williams said:

"I had hoped that the delegate from the territory" (Mr. Fearing) "would give us some information as to the *petitions* upon this subject; but he has seen fit to avoid doing so, although asked for it." . . . "He (Mr. Williams) had, in haste, endeavored to make a selection from the petitions for statehood, but found them too numerous to attempt to detail them." He "could only state that since Congress had rejected the law passed by the territorial Legislature for dividing it, more than twenty had come on, signed by thousands of the inhabitants of the territory—and these, too,

from almost every county in the territory—
praying, in respectful terms, for a State government." . . .

He further said :

" From all I can learn I have no doubt that *nine-
tenths* of those people wished for a State government, for not a solitary petitioner appeared to the
contrary, except the delegate on this floor. . . ."

CHAPTER VII

The Enabling Act reprinted—Review of the Long Struggle
—Final Triumph of the "Junto"—Territorial Legislature superseded by Constitutional Convention.

THE decisive battle upon the question of whether
a State should be formed out of the eastern division
of the Territory had now, as we have seen, been
won by the Virginians of the Scioto Valley, when
Congress, by a majority so large that it was hope-
less to struggle against it—unless, as Mr. Fearing
prayed, God should intervene, which He did not
do—approved the report of the special committee,
and ordered a bill to be prepared by that committee, in conformity with its recommendations.

The exultation of the "Junto" was mitigated
only by the fact that St. Clair still retained his
position as governor.

The bill so ordered, commonly designated in
Ohio history as "the Enabling Act," was very
promptly formulated, and as promptly acted upon
by Congress.

As this Act of Congress is so very often referred
to and so rarely copied that I have never seen it in
print, except in the annals of the Seventh Congress

(which are difficult now to obtain), I embody it in this memoir in full; and, having carefully compared the copy with the original, word for word and punctuation for punctuation, can vouch for its perfect accuracy.   It is as follows :

"*An Act to enable the people of the Eastern division of the Territory Northwest of the river Ohio to form a constitution and State government, and for the admission of such State into the Union, on an equal footing with the original States; and for other purposes.*

"*Be it enacted etc.*, That the inhabitants of the eastern division of the Territory Northwest of the river Ohio, be, and they are hereby, authorized to form for themselves a constitution and State government, and to assume such name as they shall deem proper; and the said State, when formed, shall be admitted into the Union, upon the same footing with the original States, in all respects whatever.

"Sec. 2. *And be it further enacted*, That the said State shall consist of all the territory included within the following boundaries, to wit:— bounded on the east by the Pennsylvania line, on the south by the Ohio river to the mouth of the great Miami river, on the west by the line drawn due north from the mouth of the Great Miami, aforesaid, and on the north by an east and west line, drawn through the southerly extreme of Lake Michigan, running east after intersecting the due north line aforesaid, from the mouth of the Great Miami, until it shall intersect Lake Erie, or the territorial line, and thence with the same through Lake Erie to the Pennsylvania line, aforesaid: *Provided*, That Congress shall be at liberty at any time hereafter, either to attach all the territory lying east of the line to be drawn due north from the Miami, aforesaid, to the territorial line, and north of an east and west line drawn through the southerly extreme of Lake Michigan, running east as aforesaid to Lake Erie, to the aforesaid State, or dispose of it otherwise, in conformity to the fifth article of compact between the original States, and the people and States to be formed in the Territory northwest of the river Ohio.

"SEC. 3. *And be it further enacted ;*—That all the part of the Territory of the United States Northwest of the river Ohio, heretofore included in the eastern division of said Territory, and not included within the boundary herein prescribed for the said State, is hereby attached to, and made a part of the Indiana Territory, from and after the formation of the said State, subject nevertheless to be hereafter disposed of by Congress, according to the right reserved in the fifth article of the ordinance aforesaid, and the inhabitants therein shall be entitled to the same privileges and immunities, and subject to the same rules and regulations, in all respects whatever, with all other citizens residing within the Indiana Territory.

" Sec. 4. *And be it further enacted ;*—That all male citizens of the United States, who shall have arrived at full age, and resided within the said Territory at least one year previous to the day of election, and shall have paid a territorial or county tax, and all persons having in other respects, the legal qualifications to vote for representatives in the General Assembly of the Territory, be, and they are hereby, authorized to choose representatives to form a convention, who shall be apportioned amongst the several counties within the eastern division aforesaid, in a ratio of one representative to every twelve hundred inhabitants of each county, according to the enumeration taken under 'the authority of the United States, as near as may be, that is to say :—from the county of Trumbull, two representatives ; from the county of Jefferson, seven representatives, two of the seven to be elected within what is now known by the county of Belmont, taken from Jefferson and Washington counties; from the county of Washington, four representatives ; from the county of Ross, seven representatives, two of the seven to be elected in what is now known by Fairfield County, taken from Ross and Washington Counties; from the county of Adams, three representatives ; from the county of Hamilton, twelve representatives ; two of the twelve to be elected in what is now known by Clermont County, taken entirely from Hamilton County ; and the elections for the representatives aforesaid, shall take place on the second Tuesday of October next, the time fixed by a law of the Territory, entitled, ' An act to ascertain the number of free male inhabitants of the age of twenty-one, in the Territory of the United States Northwest of the river Ohio, and to regulate the elections of representatives for the same,' for electing representatives to the General Assembly, and shall be held and conducted in the same manner as is provided by the aforesaid act, except that the qualifications of electors shall be as herein specified.

"Sec. 5. *And be it further enacted ;*—That the members of the convention, thus duly elected, be, and they are hereby, authorized to meet at Chillicothe on the first Monday in November next ; which convention when met, shall first determine, by a majority of the whole number elected, whether it be or be not expedient at that time to form a constitution and State government for the people, within the said Territory, and if it be expedient, the convention shall be, and hereby is authorized to form a constitution and State government, or, if it be deemed more expedient, the said convention shall provide by ordinance for electing representatives to form a constitution or frame of government; which said representatives shall be chosen in such manner, and in such proportion, and shall meet at such time and place, as shall be prescribed by the said ordinance ; and shall form for the people of the said State a convention and State government.

Provided; The same shall be republican, and not repugnant to the Ordinance of the thirteenth of July, one thousand seven hundred and eighty-seven, between the original States and the people and States of the Territory Northwest of the river Ohio.

" Sec. 6. *And be it further enacted ;*—That until the next general census shall be taken, the said State shall be entitled to one representative in the House of Representatives of the United States.

" Sec. 7. *And be it further enacted ;*—That the following propositions be, and the same are hereby, offered to the convention of the eastern State of the said Territory, when formed, for their free acceptance or rejection, which, if accepted by the convention, shall be obligatory upon the United States :

First ; That the section number sixteen, in every township, and where such section has been sold, granted, or disposed of, other lands equivalent thereto, and not contiguous to the same, shall be granted to the inhabitants of such township, for the use of schools.

Second ; That the six miles reservation, including the salt springs, commonly called the Scioto salt springs, the salt springs near the Muskingum river, and in the military tract, with the sections of land which include the same, shall be granted to the said State for the use of the people thereof, the same to be used under such terms, and conditions, and regulations, as the Legislature of the said State shall direct : *Provided,* The said Legislature shall never sell nor lease the same for a longer period than ten years.

" *Third ;* That one-twentieth part of the net proceeds of the lands lying within the said State, sold by Congress, from and after the thirtieth day of June next, after deducting all expenses incident to the same, shall be applied to the laying out and making public roads, leading from the navigable waters emptying into the Atlantic, to the Ohio, to the said State, and through the same, such roads to be laid out under the authority of Congress, with the consent of the several States through which the road shall pass : *Provided always,* That

the three foregoing propositions herein offered are
on the conditions that the convention of the State
shall provide, by an ordinance irrevocable without
the consent of the United States, that every and
each tract of land sold by Congress, from and after
the thirtieth day of June next, shall be and remain
exempt from any tax laid by order or under authority of the State, whether for State, county, township or any other purpose whatever, for the term
of five years from and after the day of sale."*

Approved April 30, 1802.

Some amendments to the bill, while pending,
were offered by Mr. Fearing and others, which
were debated and voted down ; and the engrossed
copy was, on the 9th of April, read for the third
time and finally passed by a vote of forty-seven
yeas, to twenty-nine *nays*.

In reviewing the long struggle, its culmination
appears to be a complete victory of unofficial citizens, won by dint of pluck, zeal, intelligence,
energy and tenacity, over official power and influence backed—at least in the earlier engagements—
by a majority of the inhabitants of even that part
of the Territory which became the State of Ohio,

---

* The propositions numbered " First," " Second " and " Third,"
contained in section 7, were rejected by the Constitutional Convention and are therefore unimportant. I have copied them only to
present the Enabling Act in its entirety.

and a large majority of those who were citizens of those parts of the Territory which were, in the course of the contention, detached from the area of the new State.

The governor of the Territory employed all his influence and resources against them. The territorial judges (appointed by the President) and the members of the Legislative Council (also appointed by the President) were, while not actively and aggressively, yet influentially adverse to them ; and finally, the representatives of the people in the second General Assembly passed a *law* against their project—and yet the " Virginia Junto " completely triumphed ! Like the battle of Blenheim, " It was a famous victory " ; and no man contributed more of zeal, tact and ability to win it than did Edward Tiffin.

While there were yet some dangers ahead, it was thenceforward comparatively plain sailing for the State party. The dangers were minimized by the Enabling Act. Governor St. Clair had not even a voice in the subsequent proceedings, much less power or authority to control them. He was not even required to issue writs for the election of delegates to the convention, the necessity for which was obviated by fixing the day for such election upon the second Tuesday of October, the day upon which, by existing law, a general election was to be held for representatives to a territorial

General Assembly. The act of Congress had, as we have seen, provided for all the details; it had fixed the ratio of members to population and apportioned them to each county; specified the place where the convention should hold its meetings, and the day upon which it should convene. The State party could be relied upon to nominate candidates and vote for them; if the opponents to the formation of a State neglected or refused to do the same, so much the better for the State party; for that a convention to form a State government would be held was now certain, and the only question left unsolved was, which party would control it.

The second territorial Legislature had adjourned its first session on the 23d of January, to meet again for its second session at Cincinnati on the fourth Monday of the following November. On the very day it was to begin (Monday, November 29, 1802), the Constitutional Convention finished its sittings and adjourned, *sine die*, after making and ratifying, without a division, a constitution for "the State of Ohio."

The second General Assembly of the Territory of the United States Northwest of the river Ohio did not "meet pursuant to adjournment," nor did it ever have a successor.

CHAPTER VIII

Election of Members of Constitutional Convention—Pro-
Slaveryism alleged against Certain Candidates—Tiffin
chosen a Delegate and President of the Convention—
Personnel of the Convention—Democratic-Republicans
control it—The Governor is permitted to address the
Convention as "Arthur St. Clair, Sr., Esq."—The
Slavery Question in Convention—Ephraim Cutler's Part
in it—Votes of Members of "Junto" upon it, and upon
the Status of the Negro in the New State—Negro Suffrage defeated by a Single Vote—Constitution not submitted to the People—Quick Work of the Convention.

IN the campaign which followed for the election
of delegates to the Constitutional Convention,
Tiffin was one of the candidates brought forward
to represent Ross County. It seems that some
animosity had been engendered between Major
Elias Langham and himself, the cause and origin
of which is not very clear, although it appears
that Tiffin thought Langham was not sufficiently
earnest and active in promoting the State project,
and said so. In a letter to Worthington, written
February 1, 1802, he says: "Langham is *now*, I
am told, a great advocate for State government,
and promises the people his best exertions. *But a*

new election " (of legislators) " *which is approaching has made him a convert.*"

Langham actively opposed Tiffin's election as delegate, and among other means to accomplish his defeat published a communication in the *Scioto Gazette*, in which he charged that Tiffin would, if elected, endeavor to legalize negro slavery in the new State, through the constitution to be made.

To this charge Tiffin quietly replied by a card in the next issue of the *Gazette*, in which he said that "even were it possible to establish slavery here— which it is not, because it was forever prohibited by the Ordinance of 1787—I would regard its introduction as being the greatest injury we could possibly inflict upon our posterity." And in the same paper an anonymous writer said: " It is well known to hundreds of people living in this Territory that Dr. Tiffin, before leaving Virginia, set free his slaves for whom he refused an offer of one thousand pounds sterling."

By the bye, if the Virginians and Kentuckians of the Scioto Valley and Reservation were in truth so generally and so earnestly in favor of the introduction of domestic slavery into the new State of Ohio, as is asserted and insisted upon by the writers of the Cutler books, would Major Langham, himself a Virginian, have made and published the charge, as an argument addressed to those Vir-

5

ginians and Kentuckians why they should defeat
Tiffin's candidacy for delegate to the convention,
that he, Tiffin, was in favor of doing the very thing
they desired?

That there existed no such general sentiment in
favor of slavery amongst any class of the pioneers
of Ohio is apparent in many facts of history; and
one of these facts is that the charge that candidates
for the convention were pro-slavery was brought
against them for the purpose of defeating them.

" Previous to the election "—wrote Ephraim Cutler years after the event—" the question whether
slavery should be admitted into the State was
agitated." *How* agitated we learn from this Tiffin-
Langham incident, and also from a letter from
Jehial Gregory, of Athens, dated August 3, 1802,
and addressed to Return Jonathan Meigs, Jr., who
was a candidate from Washington County. " We
have hot times about slavery. News is spreading
that *you* want slavery. Judge Ephraim Cutler tells
that you are for slavery, and urges people not to
vote for you. Over on Federal Creek Rev. Mr.
Pugsley has spread it all around."

Tiffin was elected, having received as many votes
as any of the candidates, and, as we shall see,
when the convention convened was chosen to preside over its deliberations.

And still he remained clerk of the courts of Ross
County and the Supreme Court ; still he continued

to practise medicine whenever he could command the time to answer calls ; and still he continued to preach the Methodist faith on almost every Sabbath day !

On the day, and at the place designated in the Enabling Act, the convention met. The following named persons were found to have been duly elected delegates, viz. :

From Adams County: Joseph Darlinton, Israel Donalson and Thomas Kirker.

From Belmont County: James Caldwell and Elijah Woods.

From Clermont County: Philip Gatch and James Sargent.

From Fairfield County: Henry Abrams and Emanuel Carpenter.

From Hamilton County: John W. Brown, Charles Willing Byrd, Francis Dunlavy, William Goforth, John Kitchel, Jeremiah Morrow, John Paul, John Reily, John Smith and John Wilson.

From Jefferson County: Rudolf Blair, George Humphrey, John Milligan, Nathan Updegraff and Bazaliel Wells.

From Ross County: Michael Baldwin, James Grubb, Nathaniel Massie, Edward Tiffin and Thomas Worthington.

From Trumbull County: David Abbot and Samuel Huntington.

From Washington County: Ephraim Cutler, Benjamin Ives Gilman, John McIntire and Rufus Putnam.

The convention organized permanently by the election, by ballot, of Edward Tiffin for president, and Thomas Scott of Chillicothe, for secretary. It was then developed that the State party, or—as it was called by this time—the Democratic-Republican party, was largely in majority in the convention. Indeed, upon the initial and test resolution, " That it is the opinion of this convention that it is expedient at this time to form a constitution and State Government," the affirmative vote (the *yeas* and *nays* being called and recorded) included every member present except Ephraim Cutler. "As a general fact," Mr. Cutler says, "the votes were divided, ten *yeas* to twenty-four *nays*"—the ten being Federalists and the twenty-four Republicans.

I do not purpose wearying or unduly taxing the patience of the readers of this memoir by referring, at any great length, to the proceedings of this convention over which Tiffin presided ; but there were some incidents, interesting in themselves, or with which he was immediately or peculiarly connected, that developed in the progress of its sessions, and which seem to me to be pertinent and worthy of brief recital.

An official copy of its journal now before me *
enables me to observe accuracy in stating them.
On Wednesday, the third day of the session, the
governor being present in the convention hall and
desirous of delivering his opinions to the members,
a motion was made and seconded that he be accorded the floor for that purpose. The official
record by Secretary Scott is as follows:

"A motion was made and seconded that Arthur
St. Clair, Sr., Esq., be permitted to address the
convention on those points which he deems of importance.

"And on the question, thereupon, it was resolved
in the affirmative—*yeas*, 19; *nays*, 14.

"And thereupon Arthur St. Clair, Sr., Esq.,
was permitted to address the convention."

Tiffin did not vote upon this motion, he being in
the president's chair.

---

* There were but seven hundred copies of the journal of the convention ordered to be printed and distributed, and these have now
so nearly disappeared that the writer, after much inquiry, has heard
of but four copies of the official journal now extant.   There is none
in the State library.   There was one prior to 1876, but Hon. William Bell, Jr., the Secretary of State for Ohio, probably destroyed
it by parcelling it out to the printers of his report for 1876, as a full
reprint of it is included in his report for that year (pages 33 to 74
inclusive).   Through this reprint it is now accessible to very many
more of the citizens of the State and students of Ohio history than
it could otherwise have been.

Mark the sarcasm and malice of this designation of the governor (for he was still governor of the Territory, notwithstanding Jefferson had now been President for twenty months). "*Arthur St. Clair, Sr., Esq.,*" carefully eliminating both his civic and military titles, was "*permitted*" to address an official body of the people he ruled over, nominally at least, upon public affairs — and that by a meager majority and only in his capacity of private citizen! Could slight, nay, insult, go further? The daily record of the proceedings of the convention were, by an order of the convention, inspected by Messrs. Reily, Gilman and Donalson before going to the printer; and this committee presumably approved this portion of it which I have just quoted.

Governor St. Clair made his address, and the result of his making it was, as hereinafter stated, most disastrous to himself.

How the convention handled the subject of negro slavery and dealt with the colored race has, in my opinion, been most grossly misstated in the *Life and Times of Judge Ephraim Cutler*. It is therein stated, with emphasis, that a large number of the delegates—it is more than intimated a *majority* of them—were eagerly desirous of establishing slavery in Ohio by the constitution. And this misstatement has been followed in that very excellent and learned work, *The Old Northwest*, by Professor Hinsdale, and indeed by nearly every volume, pamphlet and speech of a date subsequent to 1890, when the *Life and Times of Ephraim Cutler* was published by his son and daughter.

This latter work professes to have been prepared from the " journals and correspondence " of Judge Cutler, many years after his death.   In it we read, as if it were an excerpt from a journal kept by him during the convention :

" We " (that is, the committee on the preparation of the Bill of Rights) " met at Governor Tiffin's by invitation ; our chairman, Mr. Browne " (John W. Browne of Hamilton County) " produced and read the first section. . . . An exciting subject was, of course, immediately brought before us —the subject of admitting or excluding slavery. Mr. Browne proposed a section which defined the subject thus : ' No person shall be held in slavery, if a male, after he is thirty-five years of age ; or if a female, after she is twenty-five years of age.' The handwriting, I had no doubt, was Mr. Jefferson's."

Mr. Cutler is represented then to have moved that the said section be laid upon the table until the next meeting of the committee, and to have suggested, " to avoid any warmth of feeling, that each member of the committee should prepare a section in writing which would express fully the writer's views upon the subject."

The Cutler memoir proceeds to say:

" The committee met the next morning, and I
was called upon for what I had proposed at the
last meeting.   I therefore read to them the second
section as it now stands in the constitution.   Mr.
Browne observed that what he had introduced was
thought by the greatest men in the nation to be,
if established in our constitution, obtaining a great
step toward a general emancipation of slavery,
and was greatly to be preferred to what I had
offered. . . .

" In committee of the whole convention a material change was introduced while I was unwell
and not present.   I went to the convention the
next day and moved to strike out the obnoxious
matter, and made my objections to it as forcible as
I could. . . . I happened to catch Mr. Milligan's eye . . . and put it home to him; and
when the vote was taken Mr. Milligan changed his
vote and we succeeded in placing the section in
its original form.   It cost me every effort I was
capable of making, and it passed by one majority
only.   Thus an overruling Providence, by His
wisdom, etc., etc., etc."

Now, to nearly all of this story I observe, "*Ju-
deus Apelles credat; non mi.*"
What passed in meetings of the sub-committees

was not recorded by the secretary of the convention, of course; but the transactions in committee of the whole convention and in the convention itself were fully recorded, and the official record fails utterly to support the pretense of Mr. Cutler that there was any struggle over the second section of the Bill of Rights; or that Mr. Cutler by his efforts and *one vote*—first in the sub-committee, then in the committee of the whole, and finally in the convention—saved the State of Ohio from having the curse of negro slavery fastened upon it through the constitution! If Secretary Scott had, extraordinarily, failed to make record of such momentous proceedings, is it likely, or possible even, that the committee who were charged with the duty of examining and correcting the records each day before they reached the printer, would have failed to notice the omission?

Mr. Cutler names Israel Donalson of Adams County as one of the sub-committee on the Bill of Rights, who supported Mr. Browne's proposition to admit slavery; and yet Mr. Cutler himself quotes a letter from Mr. Donalson, written in 1841, when Mr. Donalson was one of the very few surviving members of the convention, in which the writer says: " I have a perfect recollection of the VIIIth article of our constitution, *which at the time met my approbation*, and which you had the honor of introducing." And the official rec-

ord shows that upon a motion made in the committee of the whole to strike out from Mr. Cutler's proposition the words:

" Nor shall any male person arrived at the age of
twenty-one years, or female person arrived at the
age of eighteen years, be held to serve any person
as a servant, under the pretence of indenture or
otherwise, unless such person shall enter into such
indenture while in a state of perfect freedom, and
on condition of a *bona fide* consideration received,
or to be received, for their service. Nor shall any
indenture of any negro or mulatto hereafter made
and executed out of the State, or made in the
State, where the term of service exceeds one year,
be of the least validity, except those given in the
case of apprenticeships,"

the motion to strike out was defeated, and the
words were retained (and afterward became a part
of the constitution) by the votes of, among others,
such Virginians and Republicans as Abrams, Baldwin, Browne, Byrd, Carpenter, Darlinton, Donalson, Goforth, Kirker and Worthington, side by
side with such New England Federalists as Cutler,
Putnam, Gilman and McIntire.

Such facts from the record are conclusive against
the accuracy of the Cutler memoir, to say nothing
of the hereinbefore referred to testimony of Tiffin

and Judge Burnet, and the action of the first General Assembly of the Territory upon the petition of slave-holders in Virginia.

As illustrating the liberal feeling toward colored people which animated the members of the convention, I quote from the records when article IV of the constitution, which defined the qualifications of electors, was being formulated in the committee of the whole :

"It was moved" (by whom does not appear) " that the first section be amended by adding to it a proviso in the words following, to wit :—*Provided*, that all male negroes and mulattoes, now residing in this territory, shall be entitled to the right of suffrage if they shall, within six months, make a record of their citizenship."

And this motion carried in the committee of the whole by a vote of nineteen *yeas* to fifteen *nays*.*

Afterward when this fourth article came up for final adoption into the constitution by the conven-

---

* It is worthy of record that at least one negro voted for delegate to the Constitutional Convention. " Kit," a very black servant of General Putnam, voted unchallenged at Marietta, and perhaps others did so. At any rate as the record stands, Kit Putnam, as he was called, was the first negro voter in Ohio, and for many years the *only* one.

tion, a motion to strike out this proviso met the following vote :—*yeas* (to strike it out), Abrams, Baldwin, Bair, Caldwell, Carpenter, Darlinton, Donalson, Grubb, Humphrey, Huntington, Kirker, McIntire, Massie, Milligan, Smith, Woods and Worthington ; *nays* (to retain and make it part of the constitution), Abbot, Browne, Byrd, Butler, Dunlavy, Gatch, Gilman, Goforth, Kitchel, Morrow, Paul, Putnam, Reily, Sargent, Updegraff, Wells and Wilson.

And there being a tie vote, seventeen *yeas* and seventeen *nays*, President Tiffin gave his deciding vote in favor of striking out the proviso—giving as his reason therefor, that the immediate neighborhood of two slave-holding States made it impolitic to offer such an inducement for the influx of an undesirable class to the new State.

Among those voting for negro suffrage, the reader will again notice, was John W. Browne, who, according to Cutler, was so anxious to establish negro slavery in Ohio ; and such intense Virginians as Charles Willing Byrd and Francis Dunlavy.

Thus it appears, the Constitutional Convention of Ohio, in 1802, came very much nearer to anticipating the XVth amendment to the Constitution of the United States which, in March, 1870, ordained that thenceforth and forever " the right of citizens of the United States to vote, shall not be denied or abridged by the United States, or by any State, on account of race, color or previous condition of servitude," than it did to establishing slavery.

Another notable fact—altogether unique in the history of any portion of the American Republic—developed in this convention in the direct and positive refusal, by the decided vote of twenty-seven to seven, to permit the people of the new State, who were to be subject to the body of fundamental law compiled by them, to have a voice or choice in the matter of its acceptance. There was considerable doubt as to what the choice of the people would be if expressed ; therefore it was safer to prevent its expression. How simple and conclusive! And yet the preamble of this constitution asserts that " We the PEOPLE of the eastern division of the Territory of the United States Northwest of the river Ohio, . . . do ordain and establish the following Constitution and form of State Government," et cetera.

The Enabling Act of Congress permitted this course to be taken—indicated it, indeed ; especially when its omissions are interpreted by the debates which preceded its enactment.

It cannot be thought by those who know how able, astute, and experienced as a politician Mr. Jefferson was, that, when he approved and signed that Enabling Act on the 30th of April, 1802, he had not as clear and full appreciation of the significance of the

omission to require its submission to the people of
the proposed State for acceptance or rejection, and
of the advantage which would probably be taken
of that omission by the State party in the convention, as he had of any of the expressed provisions
in the act. That he nevertheless promptly approved it, furnishes a suggestive commentary upon
his constantly iterated and reiterated phrases about
the " natural rights of the individual man " ; "the
liberties of the people " ; " rights of the people " ;
etc., etc. One cannot help remembering, in this
connection, the use made of the words " citizen "
and " citizeness," by the leaders of the *Sans-culottes*
during the bloody days of the French Revolution.*

So industriously and intelligently did the convention labor, under the guidance of President
Tiffin, that it required but twenty-nine days—Sun-
days included—to formulate a body of organic law
under which Ohio flourished and grew in population and wealth to the status of a magnificent em-
pire, before it was thought necessary, half a century
later, to revise its work.

After supplementing the constitution with a
schedule which provided for the transition from
territorial to State conditions, and for the issue of
writs of election by the *president of the convention*
(thus again ignoring Governor St. Clair) for the elec-

---

* See Appendix B.

tion of a governor of the State, members of a General Assembly, sheriffs and coroners for the several counties, and unanimously ratifying and signing their finished production, the convention adjourned, *sine die*, on the evening of November 29, 1802.

CHAPTER IX

THE hatred of St. Clair entertained by "the
Virginia Junto," was not mitigated by the fact that
the end of his official career as governor of the
Territory was now inevitably near at hand. It
will be remembered that as soon as the convention
was organized he asked, and was accorded, permission to address it. That his speech upon that
occasion was, under the circumstances and conditions attending it, bitter and vituperative goes
without the saying. Some one—I hope it was not
Tiffin, and do not believe it was—sent a copy or
report of this address to President Jefferson. The
immediate result was that St. Clair received,
through the hands of his most malignant and

implacable personal enemy, Charles Willing Byrd, the territorial secretary, the following curt and cruel official communication :

"DEPARTMENT OF STATE,
" WASHINGTON, *November* 22d, 1802.

"ARTHUR ST. CLAIR, ESQ.

"*Sir :*—The President observing, in an address lately delivered by you to the convention held at Chillicothe, an intemperance and indecorum of language toward the Legislature of the United States, and a disorganizing spirit and tendency of very evil example, and grossly violating the rules of conduct enjoined by your public station, determines that your commission of governor of the North-Western Territory shall cease on the receipt of this notification.

" I am, etc.,
" JAMES MADISON."

This letter was enclosed in another addressed to Mr. Byrd, of which the following is a copy :

" DEPARTMENT OF STATE,
" WASHINGTON, *November* 22nd, 1802.

"*Sir:*—Enclosed is a letter to Governor St. Clair, from a copy of which, also enclosed, you

6

will find that his commission of governor of the
Northwestern Territory is to cease on his receipt
of the notification. It is only to be added that
no successor has yet been appointed and, consequently, the functions of the office devolve on you
as secretary of the said territory.

"I have the honor to be
            "Very Respectfully,
        "Your most obedient and humble servant,
                    "JAMES MADISON.

"TO CHARLES W. BYRD, ESQ. }
        CHILLICOTHE." }

Note the difference in the form and politeness
of the subscriptions to these two letters. Poor St.
Clair! One cannot help feeling sympathy for him
and indignation toward his persecutors.

The receipt of this note of dismissal from the governorship of the Territory forever closed the public
career of General Arthur St. Clair. His biographer,
William Henry Smith, at this point closes the story
of his official life with the epigrammatic line:
"Exit Arthur St. Clair, Federalist; enter Edward
Tiffin, Republican!" Yet before the spirited and
brave old man, now sixty-eight years of age, turned
his face to Pennsylvania, where his last days were
spent, he let fly a Parthian arrow at Jefferson and
Madison in the form of a letter addressed to the

latter, which I feel it is a duty to copy into this narrative. It was as follows:

"CINCINNATI, *December* 21*st*, 1802.

"*Sir:*—Your letter of the 22d of November, notifying me that the President had determined that upon receipt of that letter my commission of governor of the Northwestern Territory should cease, was delivered to me by Mr. Secretary Byrd on the 14th day of this month.

"I request you, sir, to present my humble thanks to the President for that favor, as he has thereby discharged me from an office I was heartily tired of about six weeks sooner than I had determined to rid myself of it, as he may have observed from an address—not to the *Convention*, but—to the people, on the 8th instant.

"I cannot, however, agree with the President that in my address to the Convention, which is assigned as a reason for my being dismissed, there was either '*intemperance or indecorum of language towards the Legislature of the United States, or a disorganizing spirit of evil tendency and example,*' unless an honest and true representation of facts deserve these epithets, or that '*the rules of conduct enjoined by my public station*' were in any way violated, unless it is understood that the rule of conduct is an implicit, blind obedience.

"As the Convention, sir, was to meet in pursuance of an act of Congress, whereby the election of the members was to be made according to the law of the Territory that *had* existed, but had been long repealed, a sense of duty led me to cause the election to be made comformably to the spirit of the act and the existing laws of the Territory, as they could not be made conformably to the words of it; and when the Convention was met, I had done with it in my public capacity.

" Every citizen has a right to address that body, either openly or in writing, and that right was common to me with the rest ; and I believe, sir, it is a paramount duty which every man owes to the community of which he is a member, to give warning, either to the representatives or to the body, when he sees the rights of that community invaded— from whatever quarter the invasion may come—and direct them, if he can, to the means of warding it off or of repelling it ; and I scruple not to say that the violent, hasty and unprecedented intrusion of the Legislature of the United States into the internal concerns of the Northwestern Territory was, at the least, indecorous and inconsistent with its public duty. And I might add that the transferring of above five thousand people, without their knowledge or consent, from a country where they were in possession of self-government, to another where they will be, at least for some time, deprived of that privilege and subjected to many other inconveniences, was something worse than 'intemperate and indecorous '; and that, had it happened in Germany, where such things have happened, no man in America would have hesitated to have used a harsher term.

" Degraded as our country is and abject as too many of her sons have become, there is still a vast proportion of them who will be at no loss for the proper term.

" Be pleased, sir, to accept my thanks, too, for the peculiar delicacy you observed in committing the delivery of your letter, and furnishing him with a copy of it, to Mr. Byrd, against whom there was in your hands, to be laid before the President, complaints of something more than mere ' indecorum ' —the total neglect of, and refusal to perform, his official duty.

" It is such strokes as this which serve to develop character and, like the relief in painting, bring out the figure distinctly in its proper place.

" It produced, however, no other emotion in me but that kind of derision which physiognomists tell us is the involuntary expression on the countenance of a certain mental sensation which I do not choose to name, and never fails to produce it.

" With due respect, I am, etc.,

" AR. ST. CLAIR."

Well might William Creighton say, in a letter to
Worthington, " I have just read St. Clair's answer
to Mr. Madison, and it is one of the severest things
I ever saw."

By the schedule to the constitution, the election
of a governor, members of a State General Assembly and a sheriff and coroner for each county was
ordered to be held on the second Tuesday of January, 1803. In those days party nominating con-
ventions were not held ; even candidates for President and Vice-President of the United States were
selected only by a caucus of the members of Congress, which commended certain persons to the
people for those positions.

We learn from letters of that period which have
been preserved, that several names were considered
by the Federalists of Ohio for the office of governor, and that General St. Clair was importuned
to accept the candidacy of that party for the office,
but that he refused to allow his name to be used
for that purpose, and no one seems to have been
agreed upon by that party for the position.

Tiffin was, by general consent of the Republicans
and not by any formal nomination, agreed upon as
their candidate ; and the result of the election was
that he was chosen for governor without opposition.
Return Jonathan Meigs, Jr., writing to Worthington a day or two after the election, announced that

the Republicans had swept the Federal stronghold
of Marietta and Washington County by a large
majority, and added, "the Federalists here have
grown, if possible, more bitter than ever. They
fulminate their anathemas against the administration with unprecedented malice. Such was
their obstinacy that, knowing they could not carry
a Federalist governor, they would not vote for governor at all, but threw blank tickets."

The state of feeling which induced the Federalists of Washington County to vote blank tickets for
governor may have been general throughout the
State, and perhaps explains why Tiffin received
practically all the votes which were cast for governor; but it remains, nevertheless, a remarkable
and significant fact that in each of his very frequent
candidacies he met with the same exceptional for-
tune. When it is remembered that he entertained
and prominently championed the most radical, even
extreme opinions upon almost every public question
of the day, and often contended from a place in
the ranks of the minority, it is indeed remarkable
that he was always successful, and nearly always
without any considerable opposition.

The first General Assembly of the State of Ohio
convened on the second day of March, 1803, and
Tiffin was inaugurated as governor upon the following day (the third) and from that day Ohio
assumed position as one of the integrals of the

United States of America, "on an equal footing with the original States in all respects," to use the words of the Enabling Act.

An authenticated copy of the constitution had been sent on to Congress, and on the 7th of January, 1803, the Senate appointed a committee which was charged to enquire " whether any, and if any, what legislative measures were necessary for admitting the State of Ohio into the Union, and extending to that State the laws of the United States." The committee so appointed reported to the Senate that the constitution was republican and conformed to all the requirements of the Constitution of the United States and the Ordinance of 1787; and that it was necessary for Congress to establish a district court of the United States within the State of Ohio to administer and carry into effect the laws of the United States.

A bill was framed to carry into effect the suggestions of this report, and it was passed by the Senate on the 7th day of February, by the House of Representatives on the 12th, and was approved by the President on the 19th of the same month. No other Federal action (beyond the admission of the two senators and the one representative from Ohio subsequently elected), was ever thereafter had in regard to the admission of the State into the Union. The phraseology of the Senate resolution is worthy of notice. The committee was

instructed to report whether *any* legislation was
necessary to admit the new State ; and the committee answered, in substance, that no further legislation was necessary for *that* purpose, but that a
district Federal court must be established for it.
This meant, as I understand it, that in the opinion
of the committee the Enabling Act of April 30,
1802, had prescribed all the necessary precedent
conditions to be observed by the inhabitants of the
Territory to obtain statehood; and these conditions
having now been fully complied with, Ohio had
already become a State of the Union.

Nevertheless, although it may have had the perfected right to statehood from the 29th of November, 1802, when the constitution was finished and
ratified by all the delegates, it certainly was not a
State *in fact* until the 3d of March, 1803, when
Tiffin assumed the functions of governor, and, with
a State General Assembly in session and State
officials installed, all the machinery of State government had been provided and set in motion.

Up to that moment Charles Willing Byrd, as
acting governor of the Territory, had discharged
the functions of chief executive officer, and all
judicial transactions were in the name and by the
authority of the territorial government.

It is interesting and amusing to examine the
files of the *Scioto Gazette*, then and yet published
at Chillicothe, and notice the confusion of opinions

which existed among the people in the interval between November 29th and the 3d of March following, as to whether they were living in a State or a Territory. Nathaniel Willis (grandfather of N. P. Willis, the poet), who was then editor of the *Scioto Gazette*, on the day following the adjournment of the convention changed the *locus in quo* of its publication from "Territory of the United States Northwest of River Ohio" to "State of Ohio." Thomas Worthington, then in Washington as agent of the State party, under date of February 4, 1803, designates himself the "Special Agent for the State of Ohio." Reuben Abrams, a justice of the peace, began an affidavit made before him with the caption "STATE OF OHIO, Ross County, ss," and then issued the warrant based upon that affidavit in the name, and by the authority of, the *Territory!*

Indeed the question, *When did Ohio become a State?* is yet discussed by writers and historical societies without finding an accepted solution. That it has been a State ever since the third day of March, 1803, does not admit of discussion.

Immediately after the inauguration of the governor, the General Assembly, then in session, proceeded to complete the State machinery. This they did by the election of:

Thomas Worthington and *John Smith* to the Senate of the United States.

William Creighton, Jr., to be Secretary of State.

Thomas Gibson to be Auditor of State.

William McFarland to be Treasurer of State.

Samuel Huntington, Return Jonathan Meigs, Jr., and *William Spriggs* to be Judges of the Ohio Supreme Court.

Provision was also made for the election of one representative to Congress, to take place on the 21st of June then next ensuing ; and upon that day *Jeremiah Morrow* was chosen for that office, and he continued, by successive elections, to be the sole representative of Ohio until the year 1813.

It will be noticed that all the officers of the new State were Democratic-Republicans, and nearly all were Virginians. The fruit of their years of toil was now attained by the " Junto," and with no other concern than to perpetuate themselves and each other in office, they contentedly settled down to enjoy the situation ; yet, in the meanwhile, honestly and capably discharging all their official duties.

While they were thus engaged in attending to the politics of the State and country, and growing poorer year by year, the defeated New England Federalists, true to their education and instincts, were engaged in clearing farms, building houses and barns and providing generally for the future of themselves and their children, and consequently

"getting ahead" year by year in material wealth,
and after time had sufficiently lapsed to preclude
memory and dim traditions, their descendants engaged in writing the history and pseudo-history of
the "Territory of the United States Northwest of
the river Ohio," and its transition into the State
of Ohio, so mingling history and fiction as almost
to defy analysis; and claiming honors for certain
families which never rightfully belonged to them;
ignoring the very existence of others who
were far more important factors in making the
history of that period.*   One might commit the
Cutler volumes, and even Dr. Hinsdale's *Old
Northwest*, to memory from *preface to finis, notes*
and *appendices* included, and yet remain utterly
ignorant of the existence at any time in the Territory or the State, of individuals bearing the names
of Tiffin, Worthington, Massie or Creighton— or,
indeed, of any other Virginian or Kentuckian.

Ohio was now fairly started upon its grand
career as a sovereign State of the American Republic.   It was most fortunate that in its beginning and formative period its guidance was in-
trusted to so wise, firm, conscientious and vigilant
a man as Edward Tiffin.   He at once addressed
himself to the work of laying, deep, broad and

---

* I wish especially to except the books of Dr. Samuel P. Hil-
dreth from the scope of this criticism.

strong, the foundations to be builded upon in the succeeding years and centuries. He earnestly insisted that it was a matter of primal importance that liberal provision should be made for popular education. He urged the opening of roads and the improvement of the waterways as means of intercommunication of the people and channels of trade and commerce. He suggested means of defense against still hostile tribes of Indians, and insisted that these, and all Indians, should be justly, honestly and humanely dealt with by the whites, which, he most truly said, would go far toward securing peace and harmony with them. He laid great stress upon the importance of religion and morality as conducive to the happiest conditions of society. " The prosperity and happiness of every people "—he wrote in his first message—" is invariably in proportion to their religious morality." He expressed the hope " that the people of Ohio would assume and forever maintain such advanced positions in industry, frugality, temperance and every moral virtue, as would gain for them the admiration of the whole world." But in that same first message he refers to the interference of the Spanish inhabitants of lower Louisiana with the free navigation of the Mississippi River by the people of the Northwest, in language which reveals that he certainly did not belong to the Quaker sect of Christians. He hoped that:

" These embarrassments to our infant commerce will soon be removed by prompt and efficacious measures to be taken by our President; . . . but if our just and reasonable expectations in that regard should be frustrated,"—then with or without the aid of President or National troops as it might be—" although every friend of humanity may regret the *dernier resort*, it would be as impossible to prevent the Mississippi River from discharging its waters into the ocean, as to prevent the people of the West from asserting their natural right *to force*, with that stream, the fruits of their industry to every part of the world."

How perfectly Tiffin, in this message, unconsciously reflected the sentiments and feelings of Thomas Jefferson upon this subject! As early as 1790—long before the idea of buying Louisiana was conceived—the importance of the free navigation of the Mississippi River to our people living west of the Alleghany Mountains was fully realized, and was the subject of negotiations between our government and that of Spain. Mr. Jefferson, then Secretary of State, in *secret* instructions to Mr. Carmichael, our minister in Madrid (which instructions, being State secrets, could not have been known to Tiffin when he wrote the message to the Ohio Legislature from which the above extract has been quoted) charged Carmichael to—

"Impress the Spanish ministry thoroughly with the necessity of an early settlement of this matter" (*i.e.*, the free navigation of the river), "for it is impossible to answer for the forbearance of our western citizens. We endeavor to quiet them with the expectation of the attainment of their ends by peaceable means; but should they, in a moment of impatience, *hazard other means*, there is no saying how far we may be led; for neither themselves nor their rights will ever be abandoned by us."

To anticipate a little upon this subject: in Governor Tiffin's subsequent message, after congratulating the State of Ohio and people of the West, upon the completed purchase of the Louisiana Territory from Napoleon Bonaparte as First Consul of France, by President Jefferson, and after reciting the fact that the Spanish authorities and residents on the lower Mississippi refused to acquiesce in their transfer by the Spanish crown to the French in July, 1802, and consequently their further transfer by France to the jurisdiction of the United States, and that they were still harassing American traders and impeding the navigation of the river, he urges the Legislature of Ohio to provide that "five hundred of our best disciplined and best officered militia be held in readiness to go down the river should the Spaniards either refuse or delay to give up Louisiana agreeably to the treaty."

All this was in perfect keeping with Tiffin's nature. The late venerable Col. Nathaniel Massie (oldest son of Nathaniel Massie, the founder of Chillicothe), who was intimate with the governor during the twenty years preceding the latter's death, and who assisted in preparing his body for the grave when dead, once said to the writer of this memoir: " Notwithstanding the intense fervor of Tiffin's religious character, I never knew a man more ready for combat of any kind—intellectual or physical—than he was upon provocation. But for that matter," added Colonel Nat reminiscently, " I never knew a Tiffin who was not like him in that respect."

CHAPTER X

THE unpopularity of St. Clair, especially in the latter years of his official term, and the general resentment of his personal government, had so far influenced the members of the Constitutional Convention that they declined to confer the power of vetoing the actions of the legislative body upon the chief executive of the State, and, in fact, restricted his political powers to the narrowest possible limits. He could, by message, give information as to conditions in the State, and recommend legislation to the General Assembly; he could assemble it in special session in an emergency; he could appoint to office temporarily when vacancies occurred, subject to confirmation by the Senate; he could grant reprieves and pardons to persons convicted of crimes, except in cases of impeachment, and he could appoint notaries public. Substantially these were his only powers.

7

The value of a governor to this State, therefore, is in proportion to the affection and respect the people have for the incumbent of the office, which may incline them to accept his suggestions and follow his advice. After half a century of experience, the Constitutional Convention of 1852 approved and continued the limitations of executive power imposed by the convention of 1802.

It is only very exceptionally, therefore, that it occurs that the Governor of Ohio attracts the interest and attention of the nation. But such conditions have occurred within the terms of two or three governors of the State, and one such incident happened in Tiffin's administration. His first term had passed without being memorable or historical save for the steady and rapid growth and development of the commonwealth and the quiet and contentment universally prevailing among its people, in marked contrast with the unrest and excitement manifested by them in and throughout the three or four years preceding statehood.

Tiffin was elected to a second term of his office in October, 1805, and again received substantially all the votes cast at the election—an emphatic endorsement of approval of his administration by the people that has never been given to any other governor of a State in the Union. In his second term he pursued the same line of policy and met with the same happy results as had characterized the two previous years of his administration. The legislative bodies of the State worked in entire harmony with the executive department, and Ohio very rapidly grew in population and wealth, and its people were peaceful, contented and happy.

In the summer and fall of 1806 Col. Aaron Burr, then lately Vice-President of the United States, was busily engaged in making preparations for an armed expedition down the Mississippi River ; which project Mr. Jefferson, and the people of the country generally, regarded as being treasonable in character and purposes. By December of that year Burr had collected at Blennerhassett Island, in the Ohio River, a large number of barges and great quantities of arms, provisions and other expeditionary material and seemed ready to move toward his objective point, whatever that might have been. The President of the United States, on the 27th of November, issued an order to General Wilkinson, then commanding the national military forces, informing him of the state of affairs and requiring him to use means to break up the expedition. At the same time he sent warning notices to the governors of Ohio and Kentucky, and asked their coöperation with the army for the defeat of what he evidently thought was a most dangerous scheme.

But Governor Tiffin had been watching Burr's

movements most intently, and without waiting for
instructions or authority from the President, he
had sent a confidential message to the General
Assembly of Ohio upon the first day of its session,
giving the Assembly the information he possessed
in regard to the matter, and asking to be clothed
with power to act promptly in the premises.
Accordingly, upon the sixth day of December,
1806, an act was passed by the Assembly, entitled
"*An act to prevent certain acts hostile to the peace
and tranquility of the United States, within the
jurisdiction of this State.*" (Ohio Laws, vol. v.,
page 45.) By this act it was provided that :

"Any person or persons fitting out or arming
any vessel or vessels, or enlisting any persons,
party, or army, or marching any such party or
army through this State with intent to act against
the peace and tranquillity of the United States,
shall, upon conviction before the Supreme Court,
be fined not exceeding four thousand dollars, and
be imprisoned not exceeding three years."

The act also provided for the forfeiture to the
State of all such vessels, their furniture and equipments, arms, provisions, *etc.* It gave to the
governor power to use the militia forces of the
State to carry its provisions into effect, and appro-
priated the sum of one thousand dollars for his use
in the premises.

Governor Tiffin used the powers so given him
. promptly, and President Jefferson, in a special
message to Congress, under the date of January
22, 1807, thus states the result:

" . . . A little before the receipt of these"
(*i.e.*, the President's letters to the governors of
Ohio and Kentucky, of the date of November 27th),
"Governor Tiffin and the Legislature of Ohio,
with a promptitude, an energy and patriotic zeal
which entitle them to a distinguished place in the
affections of their sister States, effected the seizure
of all their boats, fifteen in number, provisions and
other preparations within their reach, and thus
gave a first blow, materially disabling the enterprise in its outset."

Soon afterward Mr. Jefferson addressed the following most characteristic letter to Governor
Tiffin:

"WASHINGTON, *Feb. 2nd*, 1807.

"*Sir :* . . . That our fellow citizens of the
West would need only to be informed of criminal
machinations against the public safety, to crush
them at once, I never entertained a doubt.

"I have seen with the greatest satisfaction that
among those who have distinguished themselves

by their fidelity to their country on the occasion of the enterprise of Mr. Burr, yourself and the Legislature of Ohio have been the most eminent.

"The promptitude and energy displayed by your State has been as honorable to itself as salutary to its sister States, and in declaring that you have deserved well of your country I do but express the grateful sentiment of every faithful citizen in it.

"The hand of the people has given the mortal blow to a conspiracy which, in other countries, would have called for an appeal to armies, and has proved that government to be the strongest of which every man feels himself to be a part.

"It is a happy illustration, too, of the importance of preserving to the State authorities all that vigor which the Constitution foresaw would be necessary, not only for their own safety, but for that of the whole.

"In making these acknowledgments of the merit of having set this illustrious example of exertion for the common safety, I pray that they may be considered as addressed to yourself and the Legislature particularly, and generally to every citizen who has availed himself of the opportunity given of proving his devotion to the country.

"Accept my salutations, and assurances of great consideration and esteem.

"THOMAS JEFFERSON."

This, the most dramatic incident that occurred while Tiffin filled the gubernatorial office, happened in the last year of his term.

Before passing from this period of Tiffin's life, I wish to preserve in this memoir two references to him which I have met in my reading, and which will aid the reader somewhat, perhaps, in individualizing the man. In the *Reminiscences* of Dr. Chauncey Perkins of Athens, Ohio, his "everyday manners" are thus pleasantly described:

"It was in 1804 that Dr. Tiffin, then Governor of Ohio, spent several days with my father's family while he, the governor, was engaged in the earliest efforts to organize the Ohio University.

"I have a very distinct and clear recollection of his fine conversational powers, and of his graceful, easy manners. He made his company exceedingly agreeable during all his stay in our house, especially by his entertaining and instructive talks with the younger members of our family. I was a student of medicine at that time and the governor, who was a most accomplished physician and surgeon, gave me many instructive lectures and anecdotes derived from his own experiences.

"He was very deeply interested in the establishment of the university, and took a very active part in all business matters relating to it."

The second sketch which I reproduce of him at
this period is by a very different draughtsman.
Thomas Ashe, a typical Englishman of that day,
in 1804–6 made a tour of the United States, and
sent back to England for publication a series of
false and misdescriptive letters which apparently
were intended to discourage emigration from
Europe to America, by representing that our soil
was unproductive, our climate unendurable by
reason of its extremes of heat in summer and cold
in winter, which made good health impossible to
the unfortunate inhabitants; that society, such as
there was of it, was ignorant, barbarous and brutal;
and that it was certainly true that in this country
human beings and brutes alike, coming from the
better and more healthful climate and conditions
of Europe, rapidly deteriorated physically, men-
tally and morally; and that no destiny was possible
to the inhabitants of the United States but rever-
sion to savagery, rapid decay and ultimate ex-
tinction.

Ashe brought with him to Chillicothe a letter of
introduction to Governor Tiffin, and was invited to
a dinner where he met a number of State officials,
about whom he says nothing. He does say, however, that "most fortunately for the new State, its
governor is a plain, honest, well informed and very
religious man." He learned from the conversation
at table that the governor "was very much op-

posed to the system of negro slavery, and was most efficient in excluding it from Ohio." He also discovered that a subject which lay near to the governor's heart was "the improvement of the penal code of the State, and the simplification of law by dispensing with all technical and obsolete words and phrases and redundancies of expression to the end that common people could more readily understand it." Ashe left the governor's presence "much instructed and well pleased with the time he had passed under his plain but hospitable roof."

All this my reader will probably think is very commonplace and moderate praise of Tiffin, and so it is; but it was more nearly eulogy than Ashe bestowed upon any other American whom he met in all his travels in this country; and I quote him because he permits us to see and hear Tiffin for an hour at his own table and among his own friends, although it may be only through the description and report of the bigoted and prejudiced foreigner, as all of Ashe's letters show him to have been.

Tiffin's second term as Governor of Ohio was now drawing to its close; but before it ended the General Assembly elected him to represent the State in the Senate of the United States; in which he thus became the successor of his brother-in-law, Thomas Worthington, and had John Smith of Hamilton County as his senatorial colleague.

Hon. Daniel J. Ryan, in his lately published

history of Ohio, thus summarizes Tiffin's services as governor:

" No man who has ever filled the gubernatorial chair of Ohio, possessed a greater genius for the administration of public affairs than Edward Tiffin. His work in advancing and developing the State has not been equalled by that of any man in its history."

CHAPTER XI

Tiffin takes His Seat in the United States Senate—His Course
in the Senate—His continued Opposition to Slavery—
His Patriotism—Votes for all War Measures—Impeach-
ment of His Colleague in the Senate—Death of Tiffin's
Wife—He resigns from the Senate and retires to a
Farm.

THE first term of the Xth Congress of the
United States began on October 26, 1807. It was
a special, or extra, session convened by President
Jefferson, and upon that day, his credentials having
been presented by John Quincy Adams of Massa-
chusetts, Edward Tiffin took his seat as a member
of the most august legislative body in the world.
He had been elected to a full term of six years,
beginning March 4, 1807, but his senatorial career
was destined to be made brief by his own choice ;
yet, although brief, it was a busy one. No other
member of the Senate possessing his ability to win
popular applause, ever more modestly and quietly,
then nor since, acquiesced in and observed the Con-
gressional rule of etiquette which disapproves of
a new member taking prominent part in the public
debates of either body, yet none took a more active

part in the equally effective but obscurer work in
the committee rooms, where legislation is originated
and shaped.

These committee rooms of the two branches of
Congress are to the open and public halls of the
Senate and House of Representatives as the work-
shops of the inventor and artisan are to the public
fair or exposition ; where the finished, burnished
and ornamented products of the shop—without the
chips, fragments and débris of construction—are
exhibited. In the one Tiffin was an industrious,
intelligent and skillful workman, although he did
not choose to pose as inventor, constructor or pro-
prietor in the other.

He was ever faithful to the interests of the West
and diligent in seeking the welfare of its inhabitants. He procured an appropriation of public
money for the improvement of the Ohio River.
He secured better and speedier transportation of
the mails ; a better and more rapid system for the
surveys of western lands; and urged such modi-
fication of the laws regarding sales of western land
as would, to use his own words, "guard the pur-
chasers of them from unnecessary embarrassments
and frequent ruin."

The annals of the Senate for that session show
that, for a new member, he was appointed upon an
extraordinary number of the committees, and was
made chairman of several special ones. On the 5th

of November he offered an amendment to the first section of the Third Article of the Constitution of the United States, by which amendment, had it become a part of the Constitution (which fortunately it did not, although it passed the Senate), the judges of the Supreme and District Courts of the United States would have been removable by the President, "upon address of two-thirds of both Houses of Congress requesting the same," and the independence of that citadel of our republican liberties would have been destroyed.

I have often wondered whether Tiffin did not make this move at the suggestion of President Jefferson, to whom, it is well known, some of the justices of the then Supreme Court, and especially the chief justice, John Marshall, were obnoxious. There is no evidence, however, that such was the fact.

On the 7th of November a communication from the Governor of Indiana Territory, William H. Harrison, was presented to the Senate by the Vice-President, George Clinton, accompanied by resolutions adopted by the Legislative Council and House of Representatives of that Territory, which, for the second time, asked that the VIth clause of the Ordinance of 1787 (prohibiting slavery in the Territory forever) be suspended, and negro slavery admitted temporarily. This communication, with its accompanying papers, one of which was an

exceedingly strong protest, made by a portion of
the people of the Territory,* against granting the
prayer of the petitioners, was referred for a report
and recommendation to a committee consisting of
Senators Franklin, Kitchel and Tiffin. On the
13th this committee unanimously reported adversely to the prayer of the Indiana Legislature,
and their report was adopted by the Senate. Tiffin
voted with the majority and thus again, as he had
upon every occasion of his life, he testified his
opposition to that system of domestic slavery
which John Wesley truly characterized as "the
sum of all villany."

On November 17th Tiffin offered a resolution
raising a committee to report to the Senate "what
alteration, if any, ought to be made in the act
establishing district courts in the States of Kentucky, Tennessee and Ohio"; and upon the adoption of the motion, Tiffin, Anderson and Pope
were appointed upon the committee, with leave to
report by bill. Tiffin was appointed, November
26th, to examine and report upon certain claims
to preëmption in public lands made by citizens of
Indiana Territory. Upon the second reading of a
bill to fortify the ports and harbors of the United
States and to build certain gunboats, he was, upon
motion, added to the committee which had that

---

* See Appendix C.

subject in charge. This summary of his committee
work for the first two or three months of Tiffin's
membership in the Senate will indicate how busily
he was employed.

I have gone into these details, which I could
greatly extend, for the purpose of showing to the
reader that Edward Tiffin in the Senate of the
United States was the same laborious, industrious
man that he always was in every condition of his
life.

Notwithstanding the fact of his having been
born and passing his youth in England, that he
had now become a thoroughly patriotic American
citizen is apparent from his votes as senator upon
all measures proposed which were intended to put
the United States in a condition of preparation for
a second struggle with that power. Such war, despite all our endeavors to avert it, was growing
more imminent each day, and was finally formally
declared in June, 1812.

On December 1st Tiffin voted to interdict the
harbors and waters of the United States to all
armed British vessels, because of their frequent
outrages upon our vessels while exercising their
claim to search for deserters from their naval
service. These visitations, searches and empress-
ments were made in the most arrogant and insult-
ing manner possible. British ships and frigates
patrolled our coasts, entered our harbors and

anchored defiantly in Hampton Roads and other
places for weeks at a time, for the purpose of committing them, and did commit them repeatedly;
the crowning outrage being the attack of the
British ship *Leopard*, carrying fifty guns, upon the
American frigate *Chesapeake*, carrying thirty guns
but unable to fire a single shot by reason of being
without essential equipments for working her arma-
ment.   In this affair Commodore Barron was compelled, after three of his men had been killed,
eighteen wounded, and his sails, rigging and masts
cut up by shot, to haul down his flag and offer to
surrender his vessel.   The *Chesapeake* was visited,
searched " for deserters," and a number of her men
impressed ; but the commander of the *Leopard* refused to take her in charge as a captured enemy.*
All this was hard to bear ; but upon the other
hand our young nation, not yet recuperated from
the long and exhaustive Revolutionary War, without a navy, money or credit, very naturally hesitated to declare war against the foremost naval
power of the world.

On the 2d of December Tiffin voted for an
energetic act to maintain the authority of the
United States in all ports, harbors and waters
within its jurisdiction.   On the 18th of the same
month he voted for the " Embargo Act," from the

---

* See Appendix D.

enactment of which such momentous consequences resulted. In short, he invariably voted with the most earnest and radical of the war faction in the Senate.

An event of much interest to the people of Ohio, and with which Tiffin was closely associated, occurred on the 27th of November of that year. John Smith, his colleague in the Senate, had been indicted by the Grand Jury of the District Court of the United States for the District of Virginia, sitting at Richmond, for complicity with Aaron Burr and Herman Blennerhasset in treasonable conspiracy and practices against the United States. In consequence of failure to convict the principals (who were acquitted by the jury upon a rule of law charged by the court, and not because the jury believed them guiltless of the treason charged), Smith had not been put upon trial. November 27th, in the Senate, Mr. Maclay of Pennsylvania offered a resolution which aimed at the expulsion of Smith from the Senate, but immediately withdrew it to make way for one offered by Mr. Thruston of Kentucky to the same purport. This latter read as follows :

"*Resolved :* That a committee be appointed to inquire whether it be compatible with the honor and privileges of this House that John Smith, a senator from the State of Ohio, against whom bills

8

of indictment were found at the Circuit Court of
Virginia, held at Richmond in August last, for
treason and misdemeanor, should be permitted
any longer to have a seat therein; and that the
committee do inquire into all the facts regarding
the conduct of Mr. Smith as an alleged associate
of Aaron Burr, and report the same to the Senate."

This motion was carried without a division.
Upon the adoption of the foregoing resolution,
Mr. Tiffin arose and, with a few words of introduction, read to the Senate the following communication which he had just received from Mr. Smith:

" WASHINGTON, *Nov. 27th*, 1807.

"*Dear Sir:* Just having heard that a motion is
pending in the Senate to appoint a committee to
inquire into certain charges exhibited against me
at Richmond, Va., by the late Grand Jury, I beg
you, sir, to assure the Senate in my name that
nothing will afford me more pleasure than to have
a public investigation of the said charges and an
opportunity to vindicate my innocence; and I beg
you, sir, from your seat to make this statement.   I
am, dear sir,

" Respectfully yours,

" JOHN SMITH."

" HON. MR. TIFFIN."

The committee raised upon the resolution of Mr. Thruston worked long and industriously upon the investigation committed to them, gathering documentary evidence and examining witnesses— the accused senator being present and allowed to cross-examine. Among the witnesses Tiffin was examined and cross-examined. They spent more than three months in this work, and then made a report to the Senate, stating the testimony very fairly *pro* and *con*, but concluding with this resolution :

"That John Smith, a senator from the State of Ohio, by his participation in the conspiracy of Aaron Burr against the peace, union and liberties of the people of the United States has been guilty of conduct incompatible with his duty and station as a senator of the United States ; and that he be therefore, and hereby is, expelled from the Senate of the United States."

The documents submitted with the report were very voluminous. Among them was the statement of Mr. Smith in his own defense, which filled ninety-six pages of manuscript. The matter was then debated in the Senate at great length, and many motions were made and voted upon during the debate. Tiffin took no part in the discussion and declined to vote upon any of the interlocutory questions, but on the final question he voted with the nineteen who voted for expulsion. He was a stern judge when criminal conduct was charged, and, believing the allegations to be true, he would have voted as he did had his brother been the person on trial.

Ten senators voted for acquittal, and as it required two-thirds of those voting to expel a senator, Mr. Smith barely escaped that ignominy; but realizing that his position in the Senate would thenceforward be intolerable, he resigned the seat in a long exculpatory letter to Mr. Kirker, the acting Governor of Ohio. This letter reveals the fact that the General Assembly of his own State had demanded his resignation.

On the 12th day of December, 1808, the General Assembly of Ohio elected Return Jonathan Meigs, Jr., to the Senate of the United States to fill the unexpired portion of the term of John Smith, and on the next day also elected him to a full term to follow at the close of the fractional term, *i.e.*, from March 4, 1809.

On the first day of July, 1808, Senator Tiffin's wife died.

Such bereavement, although so common in human experience, is nevertheless, to a tender, affectionate and sympathetic nature such as Edward Tiffin's was, the most crushing and disheartening calamity that could happen—at least until " Time, the unfailing healer," has gradually modified the anguish and, mayhap, even metamorphosed it to the calm and gentle emotion of pleasurable remembrance of happy associations in the past years of life.

In the first paroxysms of his grief, longing for the society and sympathy of his intimate friends in Ohio, Tiffin resigned the office of senator at the close of that session of Congress and returned to his western home. He had previously purchased a large and fertile tract of land located in Union Township of Ross County, upon which he had built a comfortable residence and otherwise improved; and thither he went with his aged mother, endeavoring to forget public cares and his own bereavement by employing himself with the improvement and cultivation of his farm. But this comparatively dull and monotonous life was ill suited to his temperament, and it was continued but for a few months. He could not if he would—and I believe he would not if he could—refrain from taking part in the politics of the day, especially such questions as peculiarly affected the interests of the State of Ohio.

CHAPTER XII

ON the 16th day of April, 1809, Tiffin, unsuited and unfit to continue the solitary life he was then living, filled the "aching void" in his heart by entering into a second marriage. This wife was Miss Mary Porter, a young, handsome and accomplished lady, then lately from the State of Delaware, whose brothers had settled in Ross County and owned, and resided upon, the beautiful farm near the village of Bourneville, which is now known as the Jephtha Perrel farm. Tiffin made no mistake in selecting this second mistress for his heart and home. All voices of venerable people yet living who knew her

in life unite in praise of her in all the various relations of wife, mother, friend and neighbor.

At the State general election which occurred in
October, 1809, Tiffin was elected a representative
for Ross County, to fill a vacancy which had occurred in the delegation from that county in the
General Assembly. He had resigned his seat in
the United States Senate during the summer recess
of the Ohio Legislature, and was now a member of
the latter body in time to vote for his own successor! It is true that Governor Huntington had,
immediately after Tiffin's resignation, appointed
Stanley Griswold to the position; but that appointment held good only until the General Assembly
convened and elected a senator.

Alexander Campbell of Brown County, was
Speaker of the House of Representatives when
Tiffin took his seat in it. On the 11th of December
the General Assembly elected Campbell to the
Senate of the United States for a full term of six
years; he immediately resigned his place as speaker,
and Tiffin was, on the second ballot, chosen to
succeed him. Thus Tiffin literally voluntarily exchanged the office of Senator of the United States
for that of Speaker of the House of Representatives of Ohio! In this transaction he has never
had an imitator.

In the succeeding January, and while serving as
Speaker of this eighth General Assembly, Tiffin,

then forty-four years of age, for the first time experienced the ecstatic joy of paternity, a daughter
having been born to him.

Moved either by strong attachment to the State
he had so conspicuously assisted in creating, and
the belief that he could further promote its interests and prosperity; or with singular liking for
the office he had so frequently held, he was again
elected to the House of Representatives of the
ninth General Assembly in October, 1810, and
once more was chosen speaker of that body. When
one recalls the extraordinary fact that Tiffin was
chosen to preside over every deliberative body of
which he was a member—two Territorial Legislatures, two State General Assemblies and the Constitutional Convention—one must conclude that he
possessed very unusual abilities for such positions;
and his descendants have the right to boast that he
was, in his day, the most popular citizen of Ohio.

At the close of this term of office he again retired
to his farm in Union Township, with the renewed
determination to maintain thenceforth the *status*
of a private citizen and Scioto Valley farmer, varied
only by filling, whenever and wherever his services
as a local preacher of the Methodist Episcopal
Church were demanded, the pulpits of any of the
small but rapidly growing societies of that denomi-
nation of Christians in Ross County. Many of
these he had himself originally organized. He

also intended giving his neighboring fellow-citizens the benefits of his medical skill. A very few months, however, brought all these bucolic purposes and dreams to an end.

James Madison was inaugurated President of the United States on the 4th of March, 1809. While Secretary of State in Jefferson's administration, Mr. Madison had become acquainted with Tiffin and had recognized his abilities. During the latter's service in the Senate that acquaintance had ripened into intimacy and warm friendship upon both sides; consequently when Congress passed an act in April, 1812, providing for the organization of a General Land Office of the United States, to be administered by a " Commissioner of Public Lands," the President very promptly, and without solicitation from Tiffin, or from any person in his behalf, conferred the newly-created office upon him, and the Senate immediately confirmed the appointment without the usual reference to a committee. Tiffin accepted the appointment and, accompanied by his wife and infant daughter, removed to Washington City*

---

* Edward Tiffin's name appears in the military annals of Ross County as a volunteer in the company of Captain Henry Brush, which marched to the relief of General Hull's army in April, 1812. Governor Tiffin being at that time in Washington, this is certainly a mistake ; and as his brother *Joseph* Tiffin was in that command, it is probable that his name was intended.

and at once entered upon the duties of the office which has since grown into the vast Department of the Interior.

With his habitual industry and zeal, he applied all his powers as an organizer to the task assigned him; and soon, with the aid of well-selected and ably-directed assistants, brought order out of what had thitherto been a veritable chaos. Explorations, surveys, maps and reports regarding the public lands and territorial domains were then scattered through the archives and files of nearly all the bureaus of every department of the government, especially of the State and War Departments; and these were all to be hunted up, collated, digested and recorded so as to be made accessible and convenient for reference and use. Eighteen months of unremitting labor enabled Tiffin to complete the work of organization and submit his first report at the beginning of the XIIIth Congress, in December, 1813.

This report was really the first comprehensive exhibit of the national domain, its quantities, qualities, minerals and values, ever compiled, and its worth and importance to the country has been very great.

The insults and aggressions of England upon our national flag and shipping having become intolerable, the long deferred declaration of war against that power was made in June, 1812, immediately after Tiffin had assumed the duties of his new office; and, of course, the hurly-burly and excitement resultant at the capital made his task the more difficult and laborious.

In August, 1814, the British Admiral Sir George Cockburn, with his squadron, consisting of twenty vessels of war, including Admiral Sir Alexander Cochrane's command, beside transports carrying four thousand veteran infantry, commanded by Major-General Ross, entered Chesapeake Bay and began the series of operations which, on the twenty-fourth of that month, culminated in the disgraceful rout at Bladensburg of three thousand two hundred American militia, commanded by the incompetent General William H. Winder, and the capture of Washington City on the same day.

In that disastrous affair very few Americans gathered laurels; of those who did were Commodore Barney and his five hundred marines, who made a glorious resistance to the British advance, and inflicted a loss upon the enemy that exceeded all the casualties of the American forces. Barney and Colonel Miller, in fact, did all the fighting that was done by the American forces that day; even though it was evident that with British success the capital of the United States must fall into their hands. Barney's marines had utterly exhausted their ammunition, and they were forced to retreat by inexorable necessity. His horse was killed, and himself severely wounded, and so the brave old Commodore was taken prisoner.

Of course, it was well known in Washington that a battle must occur on that day, and the President, the Secretary of War, General Armstrong; the Secretary of State, Colonel Monroe; and the Attorney-General, Mr. Rush, gallantly mounted steeds and galloped to the field.

What they did when they arrived there is frankly told by Mr. Madison himself in Volume III., page 424, of the *Madison Papers :*

"When we arrived, the battle had decidedly commenced and I (*i.e.*, the President) observed to the Secretary of War and Secretary of State that it would be proper for us to withdraw to a position in the rear, where we could act as circumstances required."

This proposition met with the cordial approval of each of the party, and they promptly turned their horses' heads and galloped to the rear. " Circumstances required" them to continue galloping in the same direction, and very soon afterward the " Bladensburg Races " were hotly in progress, with the presidential party making the pace, in the lead! What a glorious opportunity for fame was then and there missed by James Madison and the members of his cabinet! Barney and his marines had twice checked and staggered the advancing enemy; and an inspiring word or a brave example on the part of the President or any *one* of the President's party (whose personalities were probably known and recognized by the hesitating and inactive militia, gathered, as they largely were, from the city of Washington) would have sent them solidly to the support of the old hero and doubtless changed the issue of the day, saved millions of treasure to the government, and, above all, prevented the great black blot which the results of that day's fight have affixed to the military record of our country. Instead, the "Commander-in-Chief of the Army and Navy of the United States" was the first to fly, and thereby, doubtless, infected the undisciplined militia with cowardly panic. Oh, that James Madison had been of such stuff as were his successors in the presidential office—Jackson, Harrison, Taylor, Lincoln, Grant, Garfield, Hayes, or the younger Harrison! Then would not have happened the "Bladensburg Races," nor the burning of the capital of the United States!

Mrs. "Dolly" Madison had been left in the White House while her husband rode to the field of battle. At three o'clock that afternoon she heard of the shameful defeat, and collecting of cabinet papers and documents, "as many as would

fill one carriage," says one contemporary writer,
"and returning to cut from its frame and thus save
Stuart's magnificent portrait of Washington, she
fled, in female attire other than her own, to George-
town and thence to a tavern on the Virginia shore,
at which she and her husband had arranged to
meet if worst came to worst." The President was
at least thoughtfully prudent.

Ingersoll graphically describes the consternation
which seized the inhabitants of the city when it
was known that Ross and his army were approaching:

" The universal effort was to escape from unde-
fined and exaggerated horrors. *Save the women !
Save the children !* was the cry on all sides, yet
selfishness predominated, in most cases, over the
ethics of kinship and sense of decorum. Women
went into hysterics and convulsions; children
screamed with fear; men were paralyzed; servants
and slaves fled in every direction."

Some elderly readers of this memoir perhaps
lived in the path of John Morgan's raid through
southern Ohio in July, 1864. To such, memory
will obviate the necessity of describing a panic resulting from the passage of a hostile army through
an unprepared and unexpectant community.

Honor is due to the memory of Mrs. Madison for the courage and self-possession which enabled her to save a carriage load of state papers and that priceless portrait—if she *did* save them; but alas! the iconoclast of intellectual idols has aimed a crushing blow at this pretty tradition of Mrs. Madison having thus saved Washington's portrait.* But I choose to believe it yet!

However that may be, we have the best of evidence that Commissioner Tiffin, correctly anticipating the purposes of the invading force, and rightly estimating the results of the struggle between raw militia and disciplined veteran troops, quietly but effectively took measures to save the entire records of the Land Department of the United States; and they were the only records saved in their entirety from the torch of the British vandals upon that occasion. That they *were* saved is palpable, for they are in their places in Washington now. *How* they were saved is told by the late Samuel Williams, Commissioner Tiffin's clerk at that time, and an actor in the matters he describes. He wrote, fifty years ago, that—

"Tiffin, by prompt and efficient measures, succeeded in removing the entire contents of his offices to a safe place of concealment in Loudon

* See Appendix E.

County, Virginia, about ten miles out of Washington City; and while every other department of the
government suffered great losses of their records,
he thus saved *all* the invaluable documents and
records of the Land Department."

CHAPTER XIII

Tiffin exchanges the Office of Commissioner of General
Land Office for that of Surveyor-General of the Northwest—Returns to Chillicothe—Settles down to a Quiet
but Busy Life—Supports Henry Clay for President in
1824—His Failing Health—Is removed from Office by
President Jackson—Tiffin's Death soon follows.

EDWARD TIFFIN had but little relish for the
restraints and formalities of official life in the national capital. I think this fact had much influence
in inducing him to resign his seat in the United
States Senate. He often spoke of feeling " home-
sick for Ohio," and within two or three months
after the events narrated in the foregoing pages he
had perfected a scheme by which, with the kindly
consent and assistance of President Madison, he
exchanged the office of Commissioner of the General Land Office for that of Surveyor-General of
the Northwest, then held by Josiah Meigs, Esq.,
of Cincinnati, who gladly accepted the proffered
trade of positions. Tiffin also obtained permission
to remove the headquarters of the surveyor-general's office to Chillicothe. These arrangements
having been perfected, Tiffin lost no time in
carrying them out. Such household effects as he

9

desired to remove were soon packed in wagons and
sent away, while he, with his wife and two young
daughters, followed in the family carriage.   After
a tedious journey of fourteen days, they, with glad
hearts, reëntered the stone mansion at the northeast corner of Water and High Streets, in the little
town of Chillicothe, and were surrounded by wel-
coming relatives and friends.

At that time the confederated hostile Indian
tribes, under the leadership of Tecumseh, made
the prosecution of surveys in the Northwest impossible, and the lull in that work gave Tiffin opportunity to remove the general office from Cincinnati to Chillicothe and to familiarize himself with
the new duties he had assumed.   He had brought
with him from Washington his attached friend and
favorite employee, Mr. Samuel Williams, whose
abilities and industry as chief clerk greatly facili-
tated and lightened Tiffin's labors, not only at this
period, but to the end of his life.   Having fitted up
an office almost contiguous to his residence, posted
himself in the duties of surveyor-general, and famil-
iarized himself with the pending business of the
office, Governor Tiffin settled quietly down to rou-
tine work, and, resuming his volunteered services to
the Methodist Church and the gratuitous practice
of medicine for such poor patients as called upon
him for assistance, he passed the succeeding years
of his continued health in tranquil peace and un-

alloyed happiness. With his affectionate wife and increasing family of dutiful children illuminating his home, surrounded by warm and appreciative friends, and often visited by the most honored of the nation (among whom was James Monroe while President), his was, during those years, almost an ideal life.*

He continued in the office of surveyor-general for nearly fifteen years, covered by the presidential terms of James Madison, James Monroe, and John Quincy Adams, and Mr. Williams states that he received the approving compliments of each one of these, expressed through the Treasury Department, to which he reported upon the conduct of his office.

As I have before stated, Tiffin had been an ardent friend and staunch supporter of Thomas Jefferson. He continued to be a zealous Democratic-Republican and to take a lively interest in politics until the Federalist party ceased to exist as an organized and contending political faction, and the " era of harmony and good feeling " prevailed in all the nation, during the administration of Monroe. From thenceforward he contented himself with simply depositing in the ballot-box his preferences among candidates. In 1824 Andrew Jackson, John Quincy Adams, Henry Clay and Wil-

* See Appendix F.

liam H. Crawford were each supported by their
personal admirers for the presidential office, with
scarce a pretense that any candidate was the especial representative of a distinctive national policy.
Nevertheless a great deal of feeling was evoked by
the contest, and this was greatly intensified when,
in consequence of the failure of the Electoral College to give a majority of votes to either candidate,
the House of Representatives, by the combination
of the friends of Mr. Adams and Mr. Clay, gave
the presidential office to Mr. Adams.

Governor Tiffin was thought to have voted for
Mr. Clay at that time ; whether he authorized the
belief I cannot now ascertain. In the contest of
1828 between Jackson and Adams, which resulted
in the election of Jackson, Tiffin was so far advanced in his last illness that he was unable to
leave his bed, and consequently did not vote at all.
But non-support was as offensive to Jackson as
opposition ; and Tiffin was soon to learn that fact.

He had been subject for some years to paroxysms
of nervous headache, and these seemed to grow
more and more intense with his increasing age,
finally causing great disturbance of the whole nervous system.   It is said by his relatives that he had
suffered, for some five or six years prior to his de-
cease, with a distressing fistula upon which no surgeon of that day dared to operate.   From one or
the other of these causes—perhaps from both com-

bined—he was now fast hastening to the end of his earthly career when, on the first day of July, 1829, General William Lytle of Cincinnati appeared at his bedside and laid before him the commission of Andrew Jackson, President of the United States, making him, Lytle, Surveyor-General of the Northwest ; also an order from the department to Tiffin commanding him to turn over to Lytle, as his successor, the office and its belongings. This was promptly done, together with some five thousand dollars of unexpended money then on hand, and just six weeks later, on Sunday evening, August 9, 1829, Edward Tiffin, conscious to the last moment, and having lived sixty-three years and two months, peacefully and calmly breathed his last breath amid a circle of weeping relatives and friends.

Few persons have gone to death by a more painful and difficult path than was his ; but he trod it with the courage, resignation and unwavering faith of a Christian hero.

The faithful Williams, who was present at the supreme moment, wrote a few days later : " He has long been conscious of approaching death ; and contemplated that event not only calmly, but with joyous anticipation of exchanging mortal sufferings for angelic happiness."

The *Scioto Gazette* of August 12, 1829, contains an obituary notice and account of the funeral, which took place upon the afternoon of the 10th and was attended by all of the prominent citizens of the town and surrounding country. The editorial, after brief recountal of his life and public services, summarizes his character with the statement that " in all the various relations of parent, husband, neighbor and citizen he has been rarely equalled and never excelled. As a public servant he was inflexibly just, upright, independent and firm—an honest and conscientious man."

His remains now rest under a fitting marble monument in the beautiful cemetery known as Grandview, upon a hill just south of and overlooking the city of Chillicothe, where also are interred the bodies of three other governors of Ohio— Thomas Worthington, Duncan McArthur and William Allen—and the remains of Nathaniel Massie, Thomas Scott, William Creighton and many others of Edward Tiffin's contemporaries, close friends and co-laborers in the great events which shaped the destinies of magnificent Ohio ; and whose tombs are often the objective points of reverential pilgrims from abroad.

APPENDIX A

IT is much regretted by the descendants and relatives of Governor Tiffin that no good portrait of him is in existence. The only one taken from life is a miniature in profile which, while it is tolerably accurate in preserving the outline of his features, utterly fails to give his characteristic expression and the contour of his head (which was large and full, especially in the measurements from forehead to occiput) as represented by all of his familiar friends who have left descriptions of him.

Mr. Williams describes him as being "about five feet six or seven inches in height; of pretty heavy body and comparatively light limbs; his head large; face full, round and florid; hair thin, and early becoming bald in front; and his countenance one of the most expressive I have ever seen, especially when animated. He was remarkable for the activity and quickness of his movements." Mr. Williams also says of the miniature portrait (from which all other alleged portraits, including the engraved one herein used as a frontispiece, have been copied): "It altogether fails to give the striking and fine expressions of the features of the original." The late Hon. Allen Latham, in a letter to Dr. Comegys, written about twenty-five years ago, corroboratively says:

"My recollections of Governor Tiffin are: that he was of medium height; rather portly; large head and full, florid face of English type. That his gestures when speaking were very graceful; and that he possessed a most musical voice. The then young ladies and gentlemen of Chillicothe flocked to hear him preach or read the Episcopal service; as he often did when that church had no rector; although he was a Methodist. All citizens regarded him as one of the best of men. He was exceedingly kind to young people. If he had any enemies, I never knew of them. I regarded him as the most accomplished gentleman I have ever seen."

His surviving daughters fully coincide with these criticisms upon the portrait and the copies from it.

APPENDIX B

THOMAS JEFFERSON — STATE RIGHTS AND THE REBELLION

HAVING published in the *Chillicothe Leader*, in 1888, a brief sketch of Edward Tiffin's life—in the course of which paper I had alluded to the subjects with which this note is headed—there appeared in the next issue of said newspaper the following communication :

"COLONEL GILMORE CORRECTED.

" [The following interesting communication has been sent to the *Leader* for publication. It is from the pen of one of Chillicothe's learned students of history, and is a timely contribution. It will, of course, receive Colonel Gilmore's attention.]

"*Editors Leader :* Colonel W. E. Gilmore, in his ' Tiffin Memoir,' says : 'Mr. Jefferson was undoubtedly the *author*, as he was the *especial champion*, of the State's Rights resolutions of Kentucky and Virginia—the famous resolutions of 798 and 1799. . . . By them, and the resulting deductions, Mr. Jefferson sowed the dragon teeth which sprang up armed men, both North and South, in 1861.'

" I inquire if Colonel Gilmore's political *prejudices* against Mr. Jefferson have not led him into error? Thomas Jefferson was the statesman of his age. He was not perfect, but as an ardent patriot was as near perfection as any man then living.

He went to Europe and studied the virtues and vices of their governments, and was a powerful agent in constructing our own government. To him, more than to any other one man, are we now indebted for a wise, self-sustaining and permanent government. His ideas pervade every part of our National Constitution.

"True, he was a *State's Rights*, or people's man, in opposition to the *strong centralized* government desired by the Federalists of the Hamilton type. He wanted a government of the people, by the people, and for the people. He hated aristocracy and despotism in every form.

"Jefferson drew the Declaration of Independence, secured the abolition of the English law of entails and primogeniture, in Virginia; and the restrictions on religious freedom; secured the separation of Church and State, labored (though a slaveholder himself) for the abolition of the slave trade and the prohibition of slavery in the territory northwest of the Ohio River; earnestly advocated emancipation in Virginia, and, as President, purchased Louisiana from France. While President he placated his political opponents; made few removals from office; refused office to all his relatives; reduced the courtly manners of the prior administrations to a republican simplicity, and trousers took the place of gaudy knee-breeches. He was a model man and President.

"But that he was the *author* or the *especial champion* of the State's Rights Resolutions of '98 is news to me! I have always heard James Madison named as their author. From a short life of each President now before me, written in 1880, I make the following extract:

"'In the beginning of John Adams' (federal) administration, the passage of the *Alien and Sedition Act* by the (federal) Congress gave rise to vigorous protests from the Legislatures of Kentucky and Virginia. The latter are known in history as the resolutions of 1798-99, and were drawn by *Madison*, though not a member of the Legislature. They now stand among the highest authorities on constitutional construction. Animadversions upon them drew from Madison, the following winter, a report in which he fortifies the positions taken in the resolutions, by a State paper of signal vigor and exhaustive analysis of the reason and philosophy of the resolutions. Though few of the States followed the bold stand of Virginia, the act of Congress (the alien and sedition act) which called out the resolutions, speedily fell into disrepute and was repealed, and the legal position assumed by Madison became, a few years later, the settled law of public opinion.'

" I may be in error as to the authorship ; if so, I await correction. Mr. Jefferson was too good a man to have the sins of others saddled upon him. X. Y. Z."

To which criticism I replied in the following communication, which I reprint because of the collocation of authorities upon the subjects involved :

" *Editors of the Leader :* X., Y. and Z. are the constantly used algebraic forms to express unknown quantities ; and my anonymous critic very appropriately adopts them as his *nom de plume.*

" His contention is, that by reason of my ' political prejudices ' I have misstated the historical facts in alleging, first : that Thomas Jefferson was the author and especial champion of the Kentucky State's Rights Resolutions of 1798 and the Virginia Resolutions of 1799 (which were to the same effect) ; and that, secondly, he (Jefferson) thereby sowed the seeds of the Great Rebellion of 1861-65.

" As to the question of authorship :—Sullivan's *Public Men of the Revolution*, page 311, says : ' Jefferson *boasted* of having been the author of the Kentucky Resolutions.'

"I am confident X. Y. Z. will revere my next authority:
'. . . The famous (State's Rights) Resolutions *drawn* in
1798 *by Mr. Jefferson* and adopted by the Kentucky Legislature, etc., etc.' (Jefferson Davis' *Rise and Fall of the Confederate Government*, Vol. I., page 188.)

"Von Holst, in his accurate *Constitutional and Political
History of the United States*, says in Vol. I., page 149, that
'among Jefferson's papers were found two copies of the
original draft of the Kentucky Resolutions of 1798, *in his own
handwriting.*'

"And finally and conclusively I quote from the *Works of
Thomas Jefferson*, Vol. VII., page 229, in which, referring to
those Kentucky Resolutions, Mr. Jefferson says: 'I drew and
delivered them to Mr. G. Nicholas, and in keeping their
origin secret he fulfilled his pledge of honor. Some years
afterward Colonel Nicholas asked me if I would have any objection to its being known that I had drawn them. But I
pointedly enjoined that it should not be known.'

"That ought to be conclusive as to the authorship of the
Kentucky Resolutions!

"Now as to the authorship of the Virginia Resolutions
(which were to the same purport and effect as those passed by
the Kentucky Legislature, although varied somewhat in the
wording), passed in December, 1798, and reaffirmed in 1799.
That Jefferson *procured* Madison to recast the Kentucky
Resolutions and have them passed by the Virginia Legislature, is, I think, clearly proven by the letter of the former to
the latter, dated November 17, 1798, in which he said: 'I
enclose to you a draft of the Kentucky Resolutions. I think
we should distinctly affirm all the important principles they
contain, so as to hold that ground, etc., etc.' (*Jefferson's
Works*, Vol. IV., page 25.)

"The Virginia Resolutions were passed by the Legislature
just a month later than the date of that letter.

"But why does my anonymous critic rush into print to deny or question that his evident political idol was the author of declarations which he says ' now stand among the highest authorities on constitutional constructions'?

"My own opinion is that the Boys in Blue reversed the Jeffersonian constructions of the Constitution in regard to State's Rights in 1861–65.

"If now I have sufficiently proved that Jefferson was the author of those State's Rights Resolutions, the remaining question is, did he therein ' sow the dragon teeth, etc.'—or to be plainer and less classical, did he thereby become responsible for the Civil War of 1861–65 ? Upon this point I again quote from his namesake and follower, the most conspicuous promoter of that war, the President of the so-called Confederate States—Jefferson Davis. Note his logical argument from the premises of those resolutions : If the Union were a compact ; if it were a confederacy ; if the States as States did severally accede to it, then the sovereignty of each State and the right to secede from the Union is clearly deducible. (*Rise and Fall of the Confederate Government*, Vol. I., page 137, *et sequitur.*)

"Von Holst asserts that the two drafts of the Kentucky Resolutions which were found among Jefferson's papers after his death, and which were in his own handwriting, contained this further resolution which, apparently, both Mr. Nicholas and Mr. Madison eliminated from them before their adoption by the legislatures of their respective States :

" ' *Resolved :* That when the General Government assumes powers which have not been delegated to it, *nullification* of the Act is the rightful remedy ; and every State has a natural right, in cases not within the compact, to *nullify of their own authority* all assumptions of power by others, within its limits.' (*Von Holst's History*, etc., as above, Vol. I., page 149.) And this historian adds, ' That Jefferson was not only the

advocate but the *father* of nullification is thus well established.'

"Did, or could, John C. Calhoun state the treasonable
doctrine, for which glorious 'Old Hickory' threatened to
hang him in 1832, clearer or stronger than did Jefferson in
these original drafts?

"And that Thomas Jefferson fully understood the logic of
these resolutions, and *intended* the results which followed
their adoption, is evident from his letter to his intimate personal and political friend, Mr. Madison, from which I quoted
one paragraph above (*Works*, Vol. IV., page 25), in which he
continues: 'I think we should distinctly affirm all the important principles they contain, so as to hold that ground in
the future, and leave the matter in such a train as that we
may not be committed absolutely to *push the matter to ex-
tremities*, and yet be free to push as far as events will render
prudent.'

"In the same spirit and even more direct language he
wrote to his friend, John Taylor of Virginia, as early as June,
1798: '*While it would not be wise to proceed immediately to
a disruption of the Union when party passion is at its height,*
. . . the time has come when these principles' (*i.e.*, the
principles contained in the Kentucky Resolutions as he had
expressed them) 'should be distinctly formulated and offi-
cially proclaimed. Not to do this *now* would be to run the
risk of being carried away by the current of facts to such a
distance that it would be difficult and perhaps *impossible* to
get hold of them again. But on the other hand if it is done,
everything *further* may be calmly waited for, and the policy
of expediency again brought into the foreground.'

"What did, what *could* this mean but 'let us now put this slow
but certain and deadly poison into the body politic of the United
States Government, and then calmly await results.' *Results*
very nearly came in 1832, and *did* come in 1861! What

wonder that Von Holst exclaims, 'How can it be denied, in view of these utterances, that Jefferson recognized secession as a logical and inevitable consequence of his doctrine; and an appeal to the sword as a constitutional right!'

" I will add to the foregoing that in the *Life of Thomas Jefferson*, by Morse (Series of *American Statesmen*, pages 193, *et sequitur*), both the authorship of those resolutions and their treasonable character are admitted. And the same admissions are made by Gay, the author of *Life of James Madison* in the same series of volumes (pages 243, *et seq.*).

" Such was the man whom X. Y. Z. declares to have been ' the statesman of his age! The People's Man! The one to whom we are indebted, more than to any other one, for a wise, self-sustaining and permanent government of the people, by the people and for the people!'

" And now, Messrs. Editors, metaphorically tipping my hat to my unknown democratic critic, I lay down my pencil and dismiss this controversy.

" WM. E. GILMORE."

APPENDIX C

REMONSTRANCE OF THE CITIZENS OF INDIANA
TERRITORY AGAINST THE ADMISSION OF
SLAVERY

AT a meeting, numerously attended, of the citizens of Clark
County of the Territory of Indiana, held at Springville, October
10, 1807, the committee of five persons, viz.: Abraham Little,
John Owens, Charles Beggs, Robert Robinson and James
Beggs, heretofore appointed to report the sentiment of our
people upon the action of the Legislature of Indiana Territory, asking Congress to suspend the VIth clause of the
Ordinance of 1787, and admit slavery temporarily, submitted
the following report :

"To the Senate and House of Representatives of the United
States, in Congress assembled :
"This memorial of the citizens of Clark County humbly
showeth; that great anxiety has been, and still is, evinced by
some of the citizens of this Territory on the subject of the
introduction of slavery into the same, but in no instance has
the voice of the citizens been unanimous.

"In the year of 1802, at a special convention of delegates
from the respective counties, a petition was forwarded to Congress to repeal the VIth article of compact contained in the
Ordinance ; but the representatives of all that part of the Territory east of Vincennes were present, and were decidedly
opposed to that part of the petition.'

" In the year 1805 the subject was again taken up and discussed in the General Assembly, and a majority of the House of Representatives voted against said memorial; and consequently it was rejected; as the journals of that house will show. But a number of citizens saw fit to sign the same, and among the rest the Speaker of the House and President of the Council (although the latter denies that he signed it); and by some legislative legerdemain it found its way into the Congress of the United States as a *Legislative Act* of this Territory.

" In the present year, 1807, the subject was again taken up by the Legislature of the Territory, and a majority of both Houses passed certain resolutions (in the proportion of two to one) for the purpose of *suspending* said VIth article of the compact, which, we presume, are before you now.

" *But be it understood,* that in the Legislative Council *there were only three members present* who, for certain reasons, positively refused to sign the resolutions, and they were reduced to the subterfuge of prevailing on the President, who would not sign them, to leave his seat, and one of the other members took it as President *pro tempore* for the purpose of signing them. Whether this was right or wrong, judge ye!

" Although it is contended by some that at this time there is a majority in favor of slavery, the opposite opinion is held by many, and the fact is certainly doubtful. But when we take into consideration the vast emigration into this Territory of citizens decidedly opposed to the measure, we feel satisfied that Congress will defer any action upon the subject until we shall, by a *Constitution,* be admitted into the Union and have the right to adopt whatever may comport with the wishes of the (then) citizens.

" As to the propriety of holding those in slavery whom it has pleased the Divine Creator to create free, it seems to us repugnant to the principles of a Republican government.

10

" Although some of the States hold slaves, yet it seems to be the general opinion, even in those States, that the system is an evil from which they cannot extricate themselves. As to the interest of the Territory a variety of opinions exist. But suffer your memorialists to state the fact that a great number of citizens of various parts of the United States are preparing to emigrate to this Territory for the express purpose of getting from governments which do tolerate slavery.

" If Congress thinks, with us, that slavery is wrong and inconsistent with the principles upon which our future (State) constitution must be formed, we are satisfied that the subject will not be taken up until the constitutional number of inhabitants to form a State shall assume that right.

" It is thought to be useless for us now to recapitulate the many reasons and objections which might be mentioned ; relying upon it that the subject is fully understood by your honorable body, in all that relates to natural rights, and the propriety and policy to be pursued of a free and enlightened nation.

(Signed)   .

" JOHN BEGGS, *Chairman.*

" DAVID FLOYD, *Secretary.*"

Whereupon it was resolved that the report read be adopted, and a copy be forwarded to Congress, which was accordingly done.

APPENDIX D

EXPRESSIONS OF THE AMERICAN FEELING IN REGARD TO BRITISH OUTRAGES UPON OUR FLAG IN 1807

From the National Intelligencer.

" . . . The first impulse of indignation over the firing of the *Leopard* on the *Chesapeake* has been extended from Norfolk with all celerity to all parts of the Union. . . . In such a crisis silence or forbearance would be *criminal.*"

From the Aurora.

" In every quarter, and from all classes of Americans, the utmost abhorrence of the late indignity to this country is expressed, and resentment is aroused. . . . Let Americans be no longer made the sport of British brutality and insolence. To 'await *justice*' from that perfidious government—our invariable enemy—is to court disgrace and invite scorn. . . . We have put up with insults which England would have considered cause for war had they been committed against her, and have heard our love of peace called *cowardice*, and our submission to being plundered called *abject meanness!*

" Let this state of things be summarily ended ! "

From the Fredonian of Chillicothe, Ohio.

" To obey the voice of our injured country seems an indispensable duty to every freeman. The blood of our brethren cries aloud to us ! "

*From Resolutions of a mass meeting of the citizens of Wash-
ington County, Mississippi Territory.*

" Situated in a remote corner of a territory of the United
States, we have just heard of the outrage committed upon
our flag by the arrogant representatives of British despotism,
and feel as every other true American must feel about it.

" We despise that bully and coward, the captain of the
Leopard, who attacked a defenceless vessel. We care not
who the men were that were taken from the *Chesapeake*, or
where they were born or to what government they owed alle-
giance. No foreign power had the right to invade our territory (as the decks of our ships are) for their arrest.

" What the final result of an appeal to arms may be is
known only to the Lord of Hosts ; and upon Him, knowing
the justice of our course, we rely in humble confidence, and
pledge that for defense and honor our blood shall mingle in
solemn sacrifice with that of other Americans."

From the Richmond Enquirer.

After detailing other outrages by British ships upon our
vessels and coasts, it said :

" Our last war with England secured our freedom upon
land ; but upon the seas Britain still treats us as colonists
and slaves. Fellow countrymen ! We have yet to fight for
our independence upon the ocean ! "

From the Philadelphia Register.

" . . . The occasion has come when it is not only the
interest, but the duty of citizens to merge all differences of
internal politics in the defense of national honor and national
rights. . . . For such indignities as these there can be

no atonement but the instant surrender of the officers of the *Leopard* to be tried in *our* courts for murder, or open war!"

Hundreds of such patriotic utterances could, if sought for, be collected from the newspapers of that day, and there seems to have been no divided opinion existing among the people anywhere in the States or Territories. Yet the administration of Mr. Jefferson, strong, even fierce in words, but long-suffering and patient, still forbore to do what the people demanded, and left it to Mr. Madison's administration to declare, five years later, the war which all intelligent citizens knew to be unavoidable.

APPENDIX E

MRS. MADISON AND WASHINGTON'S PORTRAIT

I do not know how much credence is to be given a volume of *Reminiscences*, published some thirty years ago, which purports to be the recollections of Paul Jennings, who was a slave and body-servant of James Madison, President of the United States. In this volume he says:

" It has often been stated in print that when Mrs. Madison escaped from the White House, she cut out from its frame the large portrait of Washington (which is now in the parlor) and carried it off. This is totally false. She had no time for doing so. It would have required a ladder to get it down. All she carried off was the silver in her reticule, as the British were thought to be but a few squares off and expected every moment.

" John Suse, a Frenchman, who was then doorkeeper, and is still living (1865), and Magrew, the President's gardener, took it down and sent it off in a wagon with some large silver urns and such other valuables as could hastily be gotten hold of.

" When the British did arrive they ate up the very dinner, and drank the wines, that I had prepared for the President's party."

And on another page he says :

"Mrs. Madison ordered dinner to be ready at three o'clock as usual. I set the table myself, and brought up the ale, cider and wine and placed them in the coolers, as all the Cabinet officers and several military gentlemen and strangers were expected to dinner."

APPENDIX F

THE CHILDREN OF GOVERNOR TIFFIN

As stated in the memoir, Governor Tiffin had no children by his first wife. The issue of his second marriage, with Mary Porter, was as follows :

MARY PORTER TIFFIN, who was born January 28, 1810; married Joseph A. Reynolds (son of Judge J. Reynolds of Urbana, Ohio), July 12, 1825. She died July 1, 1862. Mr. Reynolds died August 23, 1883.

DIATHEA MADISON TIFFIN was born in Washington City, March 4, 1814. She is still living in Chillicothe, Ohio.

ELEANOR WORTHINGTON TIFFIN was born October 17, 1815. She married Matthew Scott Cook (son of Judge Isaac Cook of Ross County, Ohio), April 22, 1840. She is still living. Mr. Cook died November 28, 1882.

REBECCA TURNER TIFFIN was born April 7, 1820. In October, 1839, she married Dr. Cornelius George Comegys, son of Governor Cornelius Comegys of Delaware. She died July 13, 1895, and Dr. Comegys died in Cincinnati, February 10, 1896.

EDWARD PARKER TIFFIN was born November 9, 1822. He was killed in a railroad accident near New York City, October 5, 1853, while returning from Paris, France, where he had been pursuing post-graduate studies in medicine.